SHRUNK!

SHRUNK!

F.R. HITCHCOCK

First published in Great Britain in 2012 by Hot Key Books
Northburgh House, 10 Northburgh Street, London EC1V 0AT

A CIP catalogue record for this book is available
from the British Library.

ISBN: 978-1-4714-0007-0

1

Typeset by Palimpsest Book Production Limited, Falkirk, Stirlingshire
This book is set in 11.5pt JoannaMT

Printed and bound by Clays Ltd, St Ives Plc

FSC

Hot Key Books supports the Forest Stewardship Council (FSC), the
leading international forest certification organisation, and is committed
to printing only on Greenpeace-approved FSC-certified paper.

www.hotkeybooks.com

For
Ian,
Rufus and Rosa

Chapter 1

We were standing in the model village when it happened.

I was really tired and really cold. So cold, I'd been holding a torch to my cheek to keep warm.

It wasn't working, I still had brain freeze.

Grandma droned on about constellations but I was thinking about beds, warm cosy ones; with me in them.

'Tom, pay attention.' Grandma slapped me on the back. 'Look up, you two, it's supposed to be the best night in the year for seeing Jupiter.'

'But we've only got one pair of binoculars,' whined Tilly, my little sister. 'And you've got them, Grandma.'

'Honestly,' muttered Grandma. 'You've got young eyes. Just look up.'

So we did. I tipped my head back and without thinking stepped backwards into the model duck pond. I remember the crunch of a tiny fibreglass duck under my shoe and the shock of the icy water shooting up my sock. I probably should have looked down, then none of this would have happened, but I couldn't take my eyes from the sky because it was so beautiful.

I'd no idea it could be so lovely.

I stared, and as I stared, more and more tiny stars burst out of the blackness. There were millions of them, billions, trillions, squillions. How far was I looking?

Something flickered in the corner of my eye.

'Oh!'

'See that?' said Grandma.

A trail of silver shot through the sky. Racing towards us, whizzing and whistling.

BANG.

'Oh my word!' said Grandma.

The shooting star was still hurtling our way, even though it sounded like it had hit something pretty hard.

'Wish!' shouted Tilly.

'No, don't – not on this one,' said Grandma.

But it had already disappeared. In fact it disappeared the moment I made my wish, and something clattered near the model castle.

'I shouldn't bother looking,' said Grandma, a bit quickly.

'I expect it landed in the sea, dears. Just as well, it'll be sizzling hot.'

'No, Grandma – I'm sure it's in the model village,' I shouted, running off through the knee-high houses, shining my torch at the ground. I checked the village square, the bowling green and the high street. I swung my torch over the roofs in case it was caught in a gutter. Grandma loomed out of the darkness, so I ran on towards the tiny castle.

'Wait for me,' Tilly shouted, and ran after me with her torch, picking out the chimney pots.

'For goodness' sake, you two,' said Grandma, close behind us. 'We're supposed to be looking at the night sky. You'll find it in the morning. It'll be easy enough if it did land here. Come on.'

'Yes, Grandma,' I called, catching sight of a flattened line of miniature bicycles outside the post office.

Yay! Something really did fall out of the sky.

I shone my torch the other way, so that Tilly wouldn't see, and snatched up the small meteorite that lay in the middle. It wasn't hot at all, but warm.

I stuck it in my fleece pocket and sort of skipped back over to where Grandma was standing. Tilly joined me. I could almost hear how far her lip stuck out. She knew I'd got it.

'Did you find it?' asked Grandma.

I think I took slightly too long to say, 'No.'

Grandma hesitated. She was probably staring at me, but I couldn't see her face. 'Right.' She swung her arm around, bumping her elbow off the top of my head. Her finger stopped over the sea. 'There's Jupiter, looking particularly glittery tonight.'

I followed her finger. There was a really bright star hanging over the bay.

'That?' I said. 'That's a star, not a planet.'

'It is a planet, love. At least, it's a ball of gases. Amazing, isn't it?'

'But it's all shiny,' said Tilly.

And we stood there, our feet turning to blocks of ice in the high street of the model village. The backs of our necks aching with leaning back, staring at the black sky filling with more and more tiny lights, twinkling and pushing out from the blackness like they wanted to be seen. I put my hand up, put my middle finger against the tip of my thumb and made an 'O' like I was looking through an imaginary camera. I held it about six inches in front of my eye. I turned the meteorite over in my pocket.

The planet sat like a diamond in the middle of the 'O'.

Click.

And it disappeared. Jupiter disappeared.

Chapter 2

That was last night. Nine hours and fifty-two minutes ago to be precise. After we came to bed, I saw Grandma snooping about in our garden, otherwise known as the Bywater-by-Sea model village, looking for the little meteorite. But she didn't get it, cos it's here, right in front of me. And so's Jupiter.

Oh yes it is.

Crazy, isn't it?

I've got Jupiter inches from the end of my nose. Me, Tom 'Model Village' Perks, has Jupiter, the actual planet, as a guest, in his bedroom.

Oh yes. Oh yes.

It's only tiny, only a speck — really. A little bit brown, a little bit glittery.

I get out of bed for the millionth time and dance around

the room. I can't believe it, I need to go and have another look.

My billionth look.

Jupiter.

In my bedroom.

I know what it is, but it looks like a sparkly bead. It's resting in a toothpaste lid on the wonky bedside table. Next to it is the alarm clock and Dad's catch-the-baby-from-the-burning-building ancient games console; and the meteorite.

I've just tried to shrink a plastic dinosaur, but nothing happened.

I don't understand how it works.

Perhaps I can only shrink planets?

My door starts to open, and I leap back into bed, pretending to be asleep.

'Sweetie.' Mum's voice. 'Time to get up, lovely fresh scrambled eggs for breakfast.'

Yuk – I hate scrambled eggs. And I really hate things that I know Grandma's made. There's no way my mum or dad would manage to have anything cooked by seven thirty in the morning. They're far too dippy. They gave up sensible jobs in London so that we could come and live here with Grandma in her ancient house on the edge of the model village.

So that they could be stage magicians.

'Toast!' Grandma yells up the stairs. 'Seven thirty! Bus leaves in half an hour – don't be late.'

I leap out of bed again, wide awake. The planet's lying there, by the bed, sort of safe – yes; but Grandma might come in. She might decide to clean my room. She'd blunder in like she always does, knocking things over, talking to the furniture. Her eyesight's shocking; she'd never notice if she'd knocked it off. It might even go up the ancient vacuum.

I imagine Jupiter caught up in the fur balls of the vacuum cleaner, jostling with the cat fluff and Tilly's hairbands. Lost for ever in the local tip.

Or Mum might have a tidy moment, see the little thing sparkling and take it off and stick it on one of her glittery costumes or something – or worse, she might think it's Tilly's.

No way. If I've been given Jupiter to look after, then I will look after it. I will guard it with my life.

I look around for something to carry it in, something proper, with a lid. It'll have to come to school with me. I know you're never supposed to take precious things into school, but I can't leave it here.

I pull on my school uniform while I search. I stick the

meteorite in my pocket, although it would probably be safe in my bedroom, and find myself staring at Jupiter again. Wait till I show Jacob Devlin this, that'll shut him up.

'Tom! Toast. Now.'

I stuff my shirt down the back of my trousers. I rummage under my bed. There's an egg-sized plastic capsule. I won it on the pier, it's got a pink fluffy kitten-thing inside. I chuck the kitten-thing in the bin and gently tip the planet from the toothpaste lid into the capsule, and it sort of rolls up the side, still spinning, still glowing.

I jam the lid on till it clicks.

In my pocket I can feel it vibrating. I hope it doesn't burn through the plastic. So I've got a meteorite in one pocket and a planet in the other.

Yes.

And, it's my birthday in three days. I'll be eleven.

Yes, yes, yes.

Downstairs, Mum's feeding the rabbits. Dad's sawing something out in the yard. I put the scrambled egg in the cat's bowl, stuff singed marmalade toast into my mouth, slurp half a chipped mug of hot chocolate with white bits floating on top, and head for the front door.

'Have you done your teeth, dear?' asks Grandma. So I

drop my school bag, charge upstairs, turn on the taps in the bathroom, rinse my toothbrush in the cold water and make spitting noises.

Tilly appears in the doorway. 'I know you didn't clean your teeth properly – I'll tell Grandma...' I lunge at her and she screams and Grandma shouts up the stairs:

'Tom! I'm sure she's annoying, but she's three years younger.'

So I wave my fist under Tilly's chin and belt back down the stairs.

Grandma's outside the front door, holding my school bag, and snapping off bits of box hedge with a pair of scissors. She looks up at me. 'You look tired, dear. Have a busy night?'

'I'm OK, thanks, Grandma. Don't want to miss the bus.'

She pulls my collar out from my sweatshirt. 'Anyway, you can bring any of your new friends back for tea, you know that. I can rustle up a nice liver and bacon, drop of a hat.'

'Thanks, Grandma,' I say, thinking of the smell of the liver on Friday night. Ugh. I walk six steps, get to the miniature bowling green, and race on through the stupid model village.

Tilly follows after, humming. I'd like to have another

crack at shrinking, but Tilly's too close behind me. I run down the badly painted model high street, she slips past the model castle to the bus stop on the other side. In my pocket, Jupiter's spinning and I can feel the plastic capsule getting warmer.

No chance of any more secret clicks, then. Not with Little Miss Perfect watching me.

So I stand puffing at the bus stop, gazing down the street. Tilly pants beside me.

She puts on her sweet voice. 'I know you picked up that shooting star last night. I think Grandma knows too – where is it? Can I see?'

I ignore her. It's the best way to deal with Tilly.

'To-m, please.'

The bus appears round the side of the pub and grinds up the hill towards us.

I can't imagine bringing anyone back for tea, not to this house, not in the middle of a model village, not with Tilly, not with Mum and Dad, and certainly not with Grandma cooking.

Anyway – I don't have any friends. I don't know anyone in this stupid place.

But today, I don't mind. I've got a planet in my pocket.

Chapter 3

I step on to the bus, and there's nowhere to sit. Tilly's new friend Milly makes space for her, but no one makes space for me. The back seats are taken by Jacob Devlin, the headmaster's son, and his henchmen. He's the school bully and the teacher's pet. He calls me 'Model Village', as if I *wanted* to live in it. It sounds like it ought to be fun, loads of tiny things everywhere, like a theme park; but it isn't. Apart from anything else it's Grandma's.

The seat in front's mostly loaded with bags, and the other seats are taken. It's only a minibus, you're not allowed to stand up on them, so I end up perched on the end of the bag seat. I try to look like I don't care.

The school's on the other side of the real castle, and it takes ages to get there. I keep trying to shove the bags over, but there's this boy, Eric, from my class, at the end, by the window. He's got his nose in a magazine and he doesn't seem to notice. I can't work out if he's being deliberately mean or just stupid.

I know about Eric's dad. Apparently, he's always claimed that he was abducted by aliens as a baby. That was back in the 1960s. Can't be easy being Eric. It's almost as bad as living in the model village.

'No friends to sit with, then, Model Village?' says Jacob Devlin, his sharp voice crashing into my thoughts.

I look out the window. I will ignore him.

'Ahhh,' says one of the henchmen.

'Ahhh,' says another.

But I don't react.

'How is it being the son of "Mr and Mrs Magic"?'

I say nothing.

'Do you get to wear spangly tights, like your mum?'

Silence.

'Does your dad saw your mum in half before breakfast?'

'Leave him alone,' says Eric.

Mistake.

There's shuffling in the seat behind while Jacob moves into position behind Eric.

'What you reading, Snot Face?'

'Go away, Jacob,' says Eric.

'What's he reading?' Jacob asks.

'*Maths Weekly?*' says one of the henchmen.

'Hey, everyone – Snot Face's reading *Maths Weekly* – he must be soooo interesting!' shouts Jacob to the whole bus.

The henchmen groan, and Eric pulls the magazine closer to the end of his nose.

The bus rumbles on down the road. We're still passing signs to the stupid model village. I wish there weren't so many of them.

'Want a sweet, Eric?' says Jacob.

'No,' says Eric.

'Well, you can have one anyway.' And Jacob shakes the sugar from the bottom of his sweet bag over Eric's head.

Eric doesn't react. He just brushes the sugar from the pages of the magazine and goes on reading.

Jacob watches Eric for a minute. Then he takes a piece of chewing gum from his mouth and sticks it on the seat back behind Eric's head. Eric's got this curly hair that goes off his head in mad spirals. For a moment, I wonder what to do, then, when Jacob's rummaging in his bag for something, I prod Eric and point at the chewing gum.

He peers at me over his glasses. 'Thanks,' he mutters and sticks a tissue on the gum, carefully removes it and bungs the tissue in his bag. He shoves up a little too, so that there's room on the seat for me.

Jacob moves to the other end of the seat and starts poking some reception kids who were foolish enough to sit near the back of the bus.

I put my middle finger together with my thumb and wonder what Jacob would look like, really small.

First we have English. Jacob's getting 'I'm a genius' stickers from our form teacher Mr Bell.

Then we sit through Science, and I'm busting to stick my hand up and shout about the planet in my pocket. I turn the plastic capsule round and round, and I can feel the planet vibrating against my leg, but there's no chance to show off. And I'm honestly a bit scared to stand up and wave it round. They might laugh, they might not believe me.

'Tom – Tom Perks,' Mr Bell shouts. 'Wake up, lad – what's water when it's a solid?'

'Jupiter?' I say without thinking.

The classroom erupts with laughter. Even Mr Bell laughs. Everyone laughs, except Eric. He hides his head in his hands and sighs.

'Ice, you divvy,' shouts Jacob Devlin.

'Jupiter, Tom,' says Mr Bell, in a way that makes my toes curl, 'is the second largest body in the solar system.'

And I'd like to shout back that I know, of course I know, it's just that I've got Jupiter in my pocket and it's a bit of a distraction.

Chapter 4

At home after school, Mum's trying to train a rabbit, Grandma's knitting miniature bunting and Dad's got this big black mirror box he's been making. He's dragged it out into the garden, so it's standing in the middle of the model village, but luckily we're closed till April, so he can't accidentally vanish any tourists.

Also, luckily, we're out of sight of the road. I really don't want anyone to see this.

Dad's wearing braces with wands and top hats all over them.

I cannot be related to these people.

I've got Jupiter in one pocket and the meteorite in the other, and I'm just thinking of going somewhere private and having another go at shrinking something.

'Tom, Tom, love – stand in there, would you?' Dad points inside the box.

'Da-d.'

'Go on, please.' He leans forward to whisper, 'Your mum's fed up and your grandma won't fit.'

So I climb in and he shuts the door.

It's completely dark inside.

There's a load of bumps and scrapes and the whole thing shakes around a bit. Then Dad opens the door again. He looks really surprised.

'You're still there?'

'I am.'

He slams the door shut again, and this time I push against the back of the box to see if it opens, but nothing happens.

It's really small and hot and stinks of paint. 'Dad!' I shout.

The door opens again and Dad stands there scratching his bank clerk hairdo. 'I don't understand.'

Grandma rolls her eyes and shakes her head. She thinks Mum and Dad are mad.

For once I agree with her.

Before he has another go, I run out, and sneak down to the footpath that drops down to the crazy golf course. Grandad built it – on a dingley dell, mushroom, elf theme. It's awful.

I stop, just behind the gnome-covered wall that separates the crazy golf from the seafront, and study the promenade.

Right, left. All clear.

I lift my leg to slip over the wall.

I stop. Someone's rustling in the lavender bushes behind me. Grandma – it must be her. She's about as subtle as a hippo. I'd swear she's following me.

For a second I think I'll give up and go back, but I slide over the wall and run as fast as I can down the harbour steps.

Right. No one here, no one much. There are some tourists having a snooze on deckchairs by the stinky crab pots. They're not looking at me. There's the woman who always wears gloves holding hands with her husband and being soppy. The tide's out so I crunch over the pebbles and yuk and sit on an old concrete post.

I check over my shoulder. No sign of Grandma. I take the capsule out of my pocket and have a really good look at Jupiter.

Wow.

Amazing.

A planet – and it's whizzing around like a silver demon, just for me.

Yeah!

I put Jupiter away and take out the meteorite. It looks just like one of the pebbles on the beach. All lumpy, blackish, but really heavy. I pick up a beach pebble and weigh them against each other, one in either hand.

The meteorite must weigh three times as much.

Wow.

There's a rowing boat that's been lying on the shore behind a breakwater for ages, ever since we first moved here in the summer. I don't think anyone's going to miss it.

Anyway, I probably won't be able to shrink it.

I put my middle finger and thumb together to make an 'O'.

I freeze. Someone's walking over the pebbles, I can hear the crunch behind me. I lower my hand. Mr and Mrs Albermarle. I know about them, Grandma says he lays beautiful concrete. Whatever that means.

'Afternoon – Tom, isn't it?' Mrs Albermarle smiles.

'Building castles are you, Tom, lad?' asks Mr Albermarle.

I nod and rootle about in the sand as if I was making something. I stare off after them. Mr Albermarle appears to float over the pebbles, while Mrs Albermarle makes heavy going of it. Odd.

But then people in Bywater-by-Sea are odd.

They go on round the corner, towards the cliffs.

I turn the meteorite over in my pocket.

I hold my middle finger and thumb together, put the circle up in front of my eye and very quietly, I

Click.

I can feel something in my hand. I turn it round and in my palm is the boat. Perfect. Tiny in every way. It's got perfect little ropes hanging from the front, a little buoy and even a perfect strand of seaweed stuck on the back.

And it's exactly the size it was through my finger eyepiece. Oh yeah.

I look around to see if anyone's noticed. They haven't.

I lay the boat on the cobbles. It's about an inch long. The size and shape of a chocolate brazil nut, the ones Mum likes.

I think I need to do some more tests. A smallish crab scuttles over the stones.

I put the meteorite on the ground.

Click.

Nothing happens.

I put the meteorite back in my pocket.

Click.

The crab appears in my palm, the size of one of those red spiders you find in the wall.

So I definitely need the meteorite.

Another crab.

Click.

I put them down together so that they can be friends.

A pretty little dinghy, anchored out in the bay.

Click.

Wow! Oh yes. Oh yes.

It lies in my hand, perfect in every way. A tiny mast and rudder and tiny metal wires reaching up to the top of the mast. It's even green and slimy on the bottom, but it's teeny weeny, because it was so far away. I reckon two things; first, that I need to have the meteorite, really close; and second, that everything I shrink, ends up the size I see it. That would explain why Jupiter's just a tiny flashing ball. So if I want to shrink things to exactly the size I want, I have to be far enough away from them, so that they fit inside the 'O' of my finger, and the further away I am, the smaller they are.

I swing round, waving my arms.

I'm a God. I'm an all-powerful being – I've got the power of life and death.

I'm a superhero. Unlike Dad, I can do real magic – oh yes!

I may not have any friends, but I'm 100% fantastic.

Well, almost.

Wow!

'Tom?'

Chapter 5

Grandma. She's up on the promenade, staring down at me. She's got a stupidly small walking stick dangling from her arm. I try really hard to look innocent, which probably makes me look guiltier.

'Tom, love – time for tea,' she says. 'Kidney and chard casserole. But just pop with me a second to get some horseradish sauce from the shop.'

She's staring at me as if I might explode or something.

'OK, Grandma, just wanted some pebbles and stuff for my model railway.' Oh yes, very quick thinking.

I rummage about on the beach, and try to bury the boats in my pocket. They don't really fit, though, so I grab a load of seaweed from the beach and fold the boats inside. Then I pick up some shiny black stones and rest them on top.

She looks at me doubtfully as I clamber up from the beach to the promenade. She's peering at my pile of stones, so I hold them closer. I hope the mast isn't sticking out or anything.

'Do, hurry up, Tom. There's a cloud coming over. Looks like rain.'

Tap, step; tap, step.

You can hear her coming for miles.

I follow her just close enough for her to know I'm there, and I hope, just far enough away for no one to think I'm related. It's not that I don't like Grandma – it's more that she really scares me. I've never even seen her cross, but I'm sure it isn't nice.

In the shop, a man with curly red hair and very thick glasses is loading the shelves. He's kind of lopsided, like half of him's bigger than the other half. It's Eric's dad. He sees Grandma and turns, his face full of joy.

'Amalthea,' he says.

'Colin,' says Grandma. 'Have you any horseradish?'

'I do – but I'm watching the sky, Amalthea. I'm waiting.'

'Are you, dear?'

'For Them – it must be Them.'

'Yes, dear.'

'They've taken Jupiter. It's a sign.'

Grandma catches my eye. I put on my absolutely most innocent expression. I really don't want her finding out about Jupiter.

'Anyway – horseradish, Colin, dear.'

He searches around, in a weird and floaty way. Dancing the jars on the shelf. 'Wouldn't you rather have this wasabi and ginseng paste? It's made by Karma Imports – de-licious.'

'No, dear. Horseradish will be lovely.'

No wonder Eric has such odd sandwiches.

He finds a jar of horseradish and slides it on to the counter, and at the same time leaps a wild pirouette that would put Tilly to shame. Then he swings round to look at me.

'And did you want anything, Grandson of Amalthea?'

'No – I'm not looking for anything. Although, have you got a spare carrier bag, for my stones?'

He stares at me, his eyes wide and a bit scary.

'We're all searching. Whether or not we know it. We're all on a journey.' He hands a tired supermarket carrier over the counter, pinning me with his eyes the whole time. 'But, Grandson of Amalthea, you are just a child. You have a long way to travel – here, feel free to use this bag.'

'Thanks,' I mumble, trying to slip the mess of weed

and boats and stones into the bag without Grandma noticing.

I think we've finished, but suddenly he's talking again. His long finger shoots across the counter and jabs my pile of pebbles. 'Remember, some stones hold great and unthought-of powers, more than you can imagine – and here, Tom, in this village, the Veil is thin.'

'Is it?' I ask, wondering what on earth he means.

'Oh yes, Tom.' He looks away and wipes the counter down. 'This village, Bywater-by-Sea, has astral connections you can only dream of.'

Outside the shop Grandma stops to put a plastic bag on her head, to keep the occasional spots of rain from her bird's nest hairdo.

'Thing is, Tom, dear, Colin is short of a synapse or two – but I feel a little responsible, so treat him kindly. For my sake.'

We walk back to the model village together, while I ponder how Grandma could possibly be responsible for the madness that is Eric's dad.

Chapter 6

Did you know, dolls' lifebelts sink?

I know it, because Tilly's playing in the bathroom wash-basin with her rubbish little Woodland Friends animals, and baby otter is drowning because of his lifebelt. He floats, but it doesn't. She doesn't seem to have noticed. I reach my hand out, to rescue him.

'NO!' she shouts. 'YOU MAY NOT PLAY WITH MY WOODLAND FRIENDS.'

'I was only trying to save him.'

'Well, don't – I'd rather he drowned.' And then she turns to me. 'Do you want to play? We could play Woodland Friends star troopers if you like.'

'What, now?'

She nods.

I probably just stare at her.

'Poo,' she says, plunging baby otter deep under the water. 'You never play with me.'

I slip back out of the bathroom. For a moment, I had thought of showing her the dinghy and the boat, but there's nothing like being shouted at to stop you wanting to share with someone.

I've got a stomach ache. Grandma's kidney casserole was disgusting. Dad was the only one who ate it. Mum made polite noises and ran off to get some crackers. I wish we could have fish fingers. Grandma makes what she calls 'proper food' all the time, with weird bits of meat that no sensible person would ever buy.

We had semolina for pudding. Actually, it was quite nice, but I wasn't going to admit it.

Tilly and I are supposed to have gone to bed.

From my bedroom, I gaze over the bay. There's a small storm cloud floating right over the harbour. It's tiny, like someone painted it there. A man on the shore's waving at it. Some people are weird. And in this village, they're even weirder.

In the distance are some sheep, and next to them are some cows, and Mr Burdock's donkey. And a squirrel on the monkey puzzle tree.

They'd be dead cute small.

I don't even think about it.

Click,

Click,

Click,

Click,

Click,

Click.

'Eeyore,' squeaks the donkey and poos on the carpet.

Yay!

The tiny animals race round the floor, nuzzling at the carpet as if they could eat it. They're really cute, but I think they're also really hungry.

Oh dear, I hadn't thought about that. They'll need something to eat. Grass? I chase them around the room and more tiny poos appear on the carpet.

I'd forgotten they could poo.

I corner a sheep, catching him with a glass and a piece of paper. He's like a motorised piece of popcorn racing round and round, but I can't keep him in a glass.

I catch them one by one and collect them together in the lid of a box. Now I've got three pieces of popcorn running about. I trap the cows and donkey between my school shoes and drop them in the box. The squirrel's run away already. I suppose squirrels don't really mix with sheep and cows. I worry about its disappearance for about a nanosecond and address the problem of grass.

It's nearly dark, but so warm all the doors and windows are open. I slip out on to the landing, and tiptoe down the stairs. Dad's stringing silk handkerchiefs together, and Mum's flicking through playing cards.

'Hello, Tom, love,' she says, calling me into the sitting room. 'Everything all right?'

'Yes, Mum.'

'Lovely living here, isn't it – the sea on your doorstep.' She smiles and strokes my hair.

I think of the skanky beach, the tar blobs on the pebbles, the stink of dead fish. 'Yes, lovely.'

'Pick a card?'

Mum holds out the cards. I pick one. Ace of diamonds.

'Now.' Mum closes her eyes and waves her hands about. 'Eight of clubs, you've got the eight of clubs.'

'No,' I say, turning the card round so that she can see it.

'You've got the ace of diamonds?' She looks puzzled. 'I don't understand, you shouldn't have – what's gone wrong?'

I leave Mum staring at the pile of cards, and sneak over to the French windows.

No sign of Grandma.

I slip through, into the garden. Behind the miniature bowling green is a miniature meadow. I grab some handfuls of grass and swing round to run back into the house. But Grandma's standing in the doorway, looking expectant.

I hang on to the grass, though I'd like to drop it. 'For Tilly's Woodland Friends,' I say, and charge past.

But I notice that she's got my school bag, with all the pockets undone, as if she's looking for something.

Chapter 7

I get up early and shrink a model dinosaur. It's really small, so I put it in the capsule with Jupiter.

'Baa.'

My little animals are racing round their pen, so I give them some more grass and hide them under the bed.

Mum's trying on a pumpkin suit.

'What d'you think, Tom?'

It's not a good look. 'Lovely, Mum.'

They're doing a Halloween performance in the town hall tonight. I wish they wouldn't.

Grandma's putting saucepans away, noisily. The man on the radio's droning on about something, but with Grandma crashing about, I can't really hear. My breakfast is cereal from a cracked bowl, eaten with a serving spoon which might once have had a silver coating, but is all scratchy and coppery now. It's too big for my mouth and tastes weird.

'...*And we're going over live to our reporter, John King at the University of Manchester...*'

Crash. Grandma drops the roasting pan.

'So, Tom, dear – the other night – when we saw the shooting star...'

'...*from the Jodrell Bank research centre, of course where...*'

'Yes, Grandma?'

'Did you actually...wish?'

Bang. She slams the kitchen door and scrapes the coal scuttle across the yard.

'...*scientists have been working through the night to establish the pattern of events leading up to the disappearance of...*'

Bang, crash. She drags it back into the kitchen.

'No,' I lie.

She stares at me, as if the lie's written all over my face. I feel a blush creep up my neck.

Dad bursts in through the kitchen door with a large sheet of plywood. 'Have a good day, Tom. Clean your teeth.'

'Thanks, Dad.' I stuff the last spoon of cereal sludge into my mouth and run.

There's a sort of scuffling on the landing when I get to the top of the stairs, but I can't see any sign of invasion in my bedroom. I've got the meteorite, safe in my pocket, and the boats are sitting on the windowsill. They seem a bit bigger than I remember. I take the mast out of the dinghy and bung them both in my trouser pocket. I pull the box out from under the bed. The tiny sheep nuzzle the pile of grass I picked last night. The cows chew my hairbrush. The donkey's more of a problem – he keeps making this awful noise, so I shut him in the toy garage with a pinch of grass.

'Eeyore.'

There are loads of tiny poos all over the place.

'Shh. I'll take you all out later, for a stroll in the model village, but you'll have to wait until I've been to school.' I feel a bit daft talking to the animals, but Tilly does it all the time, and hers are made of plastic.

I dash out of the door and remember Jupiter. Is it safer here or with me?

I glance back in the room. The capsule's lying in the middle of the floor. I'd better take it, just in case.

I'm at the bus stop before Tilly, so I take a moment to look at Jupiter. I click open the capsule but Jupiter's stopped spinning. It's nestling by the dinosaur's tail and it's not a lovely little twinkling star any more – it's more like a brown ball, lying still at the bottom of the capsule. I prod it, and it rolls round the capsule, just like a bead would.

My mouth goes dry. This is not good, surely this is not good. Jupiter is a major part of our solar system and I seem to have killed it. I roll it round the little egg-shaped pod again – perhaps if I can get it spinning fast enough it'll do the glittery thing again.

I roll it faster. Perhaps it's the wrong way?

I roll it the other way. Perhaps that's the wrong way?

I peer in again. It's not even spinning a little bit.

I hold the meteorite next to the capsule – perhaps it'll make it come back to life.

'Oh, Tom, there you are.' It's Grandma. I should have heard her walking stick on the path. I should have shut the capsule faster, because Tilly's right there at my elbow smiling like a cat.

I stuff everything back in my pockets, the lid half on the pod, and try to look innocent. Tilly's smile gets smugger. I poke her, she makes an exaggerated moan.

'Tom, love, stop it – come on, act your age, not like a four-year-old.'

I stick my tongue out at Tilly: she does the smile again. I could wring her neck.

She jumps on the bus next to Milly.

And I turn the dead planet over in my pocket.

Chapter 8

Mr Bell only has one volume. Loud.

Jacob Devlin giggles all through registration, and Mr Bell ignores it, shouting at the rest of us instead. The classroom's too hot. Everywhere's too hot today. It's more like June than the end of October. Mr Bell gets louder, and I get hotter.

I'm longing for someone to turn the radiators off, but instead, the teaching assistant props the windows open. It doesn't make any difference, it's still boiling.

Mr Bell wants us all to get on with cutting out pumpkin lanterns. He wants us to work as a team. Apparently:

Together

Everyone

Achieves

More.

I don't quite know how more people waiting to use the same knife on a pile of pumpkins can achieve more, but Mr Bell seems very excited about it.

He hands them out to everybody, but it turns out he's only bought twenty-nine pumpkins, not thirty. He's forgotten about me, so I can't work as a team, I can't achieve more. Good, I don't think I could concentrate on cutting one out.

'Mr Bell, sir, can I go on the computer?' I ask.

He says yes, because he's having a moment with Eric. Eric's face would be white if it wasn't covered in snot.

My back's to the wall, so no one can see what I'm doing. I get the internet up on the screen and type 'Jupiter' into the search engine.

'But I really don't feel well, Mr Bell.' Today, Eric's face is so white that it's practically blue. 'The pumpkins are making me feel sicker.'

'Sit down by the window, and see how you feel in a bit.' I can tell that Mr Bell doesn't like Eric. He peers at Eric as if Eric's an alien life form.

Eric sits next to Jacob Devlin, his head hanging between his knees.

'Go away, Snot Face Four Eyes,' says Jacob.

Eric doesn't move.

I type, 'What would happen if Jupiter didn't exist?' I get a load of answers that I don't understand. I'm just typing, 'What would happen if Jupiter disappeared?' when Eric leaps to his feet and vomits all over Jacob.

I don't get to look up any more on the computer – Jacob Devlin gets to use it, because he's the headmaster's son and he was the one that Eric vomited on. Jacob also gets to wear a pink glittery tracksuit and some pink sparkly shoes from the lost property box. The tracksuit bottoms are tight around the wrist, the collar and the waist, so Jacob looks like a giant string of glittering sausages. He tries to hide in the corner of the room, but it's like trying to hide a zeppelin in a cornflake box. I wish I had a camera.

I get to sharpen pencils and worry instead. The classroom smells like a cheese factory and the teaching assistant spends the whole time scrubbing the carpet with disinfectant. It's really hard not to vomit in sympathy. I keep swallowing, like Eric did.

I look over Jacob's sparkling shoulder. He's playing a racing game. One hundred and twenty-seven laps. He's not going to get off the computer any time soon.

When the bell goes, I hover inside, hoping to get another

go in the empty classroom, but Mr Bell gives me a shove out of the door. 'Off you go, Tom, have a bit of fresh air. Smells like a vomitorium in here.'

Jacob Devlin's out there, giant and pink, handing out sweets to his mates. Only Jacob Devlin could get away with being dressed like a girl without anyone mentioning it. His mum, also giant and pink, thrusts a paper bag with more sweets over the school wall. I've got an apple from Grandma. Not just an apple, an enormous cooking-type apple – it might taste good, but I'm not eating it in public.

I lurk in the corner of the playground, turning my back on everyone else. I click the capsule open.

Nothing. No movement, no light, just a dull little round thing.

'Hey! Model Village, what you got there, then?' It's Jacob Devlin. He's right next to me, I can smell the toffees on his fat breath. I click the lid down and stuff the capsule back in my pocket, but I'm not quick enough.

Jacob's hand reaches up and knocks it out of my palm and the capsule bounces across the gravel.

'Here, me,' shouts one of his henchmen – and the capsule flies through the air, from one to the other, and I'm doing that stupid hopeless thing of running from one person to the next just as it leaves their hand.

'Give it!' I shout.

And then it stops, with Jacob. He stands staring at me, towering over me, the capsule in his hand. He's chewing something, his blubbery lips going over and over, a little trail of spit at the corner of his mouth. He grins, his smile as smug as the one Tilly does.

'Don't,' I say.

'Why? You got a little model man in there? Special edition, for the model village?'

I try to grab it from him, but he skips backwards out of reach and the boats fall out of my pocket.

I rush to rescue them, but the henchmen swoop by, and get to them first.

'Yeah!' shouts one.

'Neat!' calls another. They dance in front of me, waving the little boats.

I stop. I'm never going to catch up with them. For a second, I form my thumb and middle finger into an 'O'. I lift it up. Jacob doesn't fit inside. He's too fat.

He slips his nails under the top of the capsule. I step back, and join both my hands together, my two thumbs touching, my two middle fingers making an arch. He fits inside my fingers now. I could just click.

But I don't.

And he pops the lid off.

He peers inside. Then looks up at his adoring fans. 'Ah, bless. Model Village Perks has brought an ickle tiny dinosaur to school with him today. Was that for show and tell? Ahhhh.'

'No – it's not that...' I step towards him.

He dances backwards. 'Scared I might want to keep it? Oh no, I won't do that – I won't steal your precious little dinosaur. I wouldn't do such a nasty thing.'

And grinning at the crowd, he empties the capsule on to the gravel, and grinds everything under his shoe.

Chapter 9

I think they call it seeing red. I think that the things I did to Jacob this morning were only natural. I know I jumped on him, bounced off his huge belly, shouted at him, and tried to tear his ear off. I certainly hooked my fingers into his nostrils and pulled as hard as I could. It all hurt a lot.

There was this bit when my ears filled with a roaring noise – it might have been in my head, or it might have been everyone else screaming at us. Somehow he kicked me in the jaw, but it just made me angrier and that's probably when I bit his nose.

That'll be why I ended up here in the office corridor, alone, except for Eric, who's leaning over a sick bowl. Mr Bell let Jacob off. He even gave him a piece of cake from the staffroom. I wish I'd shrunk him. I wish I'd shrunk both of them.

I could shrink Eric's sick bowl, then it wouldn't smell so bad.

Eric's mumbling, so I lean forward to listen. It's a mistake; he stinks of Parmesan.

'Dad told the school nurse I was sick because the solar system's sick.'

'Say that again?'

'I'm sure it's the chickpea fritters, but Dad told the nurse it's because the planets are out of alignment. Because Jupiter's been stolen.'

The headmaster's door swings open. Mr Devlin sticks his head out, sees Eric, sees me and goes back in.

'Because he was abducted by aliens as a toddler,' Eric says. 'Apparently, it's made me really sensitive to planetary change.'

'Really?'

'He's sort of right – the planets *are* out of alignment. With Jupiter gone, there's nothing to hold the rest of them in line. The Earth's moving towards the sun already – they can all hurtle towards the sun. 'S'a disaster,' says Eric, swallowing hard. His face is white with green snot and tiny bits of dried carrot now. It matches his hair.

'Is it?'

'Yeah, without Jupiter, we're –' And he vomits into the bowl.

He barely stops. 'Yeah the whole solar system's kept in place by Jupiter and the sun, pulling in different directions. That's why it's getting really warm.'

'Oh?'

'Yeah, we're getting closer to the sun. And the Asteroid Belt will go mad without Jupiter. There's nothing to stop stuff from that crashing into us, and ultimately…'

Behind us, the door to the street swings open. Eric's dad, Colin, stands in the doorway. They look exactly the same, but Colin's bigger, lopsided and got less snot and carrot on his face.

'Eric, sweetheart – a bit under the weather?'

'Ultimately what?' I ask.

But Eric doesn't answer, just throws up over his father's trousers and staggers out.

Chapter 10

I'm beginning to wonder if shrinking Jupiter was such a good thing. At the end of school I get to look for it in the playground. Fat chance – a thing the size and colour of a lentil in a gravel football pitch?

The boats are gone and someone's stolen the dinosaur.

I walk home, and to make myself feel better I do a bit more shrinking. Just a little bit. Nothing serious.

A bench,

Click.

The large plastic hot dog outside the chip shop, which Mum hates,

Click.

A sand sculpture of the Prime Minister,

Click. It dissolves in my hand.

I stop for a moment. Mr and Mrs Albermarle go past.

He's ever so tall, and she seems to be holding on to his coat as if he might run away.

Once they've gone, I look around for more things to shrink.

A pumpkin lantern from outside the pub,

Click.

Another pumpkin lantern,

Click.

It's getting dark, so the pumpkin lanterns look really cute, about the size of cherry tomatoes, but glowing. I take four more.

Click, click, click, click.

Oh yes! I line them up on the sea wall and put the bench at the end. The bench is completely perfect in every way. It's even got a tiny drinks can scrumpled into the back.

Something whooshes over my head.

And another, and another.

Whoosh.

Whoosh.

Whoosh.

Shooting stars, masses of them.

Wow. Like fireworks.

They're going off all the time.

Awesome.

I blow out the candles in the pumpkin lanterns and put them gently into my backpack. The bench just fits on top with the plastic hot dog. Perhaps I'll give these to Tilly.

Eric's dad scuttles along the road. He's got a massive roll of wire that he's laying out behind him.

'Oh – evening, Grandson of Amalthea.'

I nod. I really don't know what to say to him.

He points up at the shooting stars. 'They're coming, Tom. Won't be long.' And he runs on, paying out his wire.

A band of trick or treaters career by, and I tuck myself in against a wall. Eric's hanging around at the back. I can tell it's him – even with make-up, no one has a face that white. He doesn't look very happy.

If I'd been sick at school, Grandma would never let me out, but I suppose that with a dad like Eric's anything goes.

They disappear around the corner. I wonder what the time is? I'd like to see the news, but I don't want to go anywhere near home, or the town hall, not with Mum dressed in a pumpkin suit. Who knows what Dad's dressed as – Frankenstein?

I hope nobody goes to 'Mr and Mrs Magic's Night of Halloween Fun'. I hope it's a disaster and they give up and we can go back to London.

I cross the square and peer into the penny arcade. The

man in the booth is watching the telly. There's a shot of London Zoo, and a picture of a polar bear, then a reporter stands by a big crater, and I can see that the wall of the zoo's disappeared. They show a tiny piece of rock, and some men in white all-in-one suit things and a load of zookeepers running around with torches looking in the trees. Then a red-faced man with a penguin under his arm starts talking to the camera.

Then they show a picture of the Eiffel Tower, with a chunk missing.

Then they show a map of the solar system with Jupiter missing.

It's all my fault.

I'm going to destroy the planet and there's nothing I can do about it.

I feel 100% rubbish.

Then I feel 100% angry. It's not all my fault – some of it's Jacob Devlin's fault. He was the one that emptied Jupiter out on to the playground.

I'll go home. Watch the news. Maybe tell Mum later?

I turn to go back to the house, but something's clattering on the street. Someone's dragging something.

Grandma's stick?

Again?

Chapter 11

But it's not Grandma. It's something huge, with a stick pushing something smaller along the road. The smaller thing's whimpering.

I shrink back against the wall.

The huge thing's Jacob Devlin, and the whimpering thing's Eric. Jacob's got a plastic toasting fork in his hand, and he's pressing it into Eric's back. Jacob's wearing a shiny red plastic devil's costume. Even in the near dark I can see that it's meant for a much smaller person.

'Right, Snot Face Geek…'

'My name's Eric.'

'My name's Eric. So?' He jabs at Eric.

'So leave me alone.'

'I might, if you give me all your sweets.'

'But I haven't got any.'

'All right then, if you can't give me your sweets, then I've got something for you. After all, you barfed on me – you "very kindly" gave me your breakfast. I want to give you something back, so I think I'll give you my dinner.'

'What?' The pumpkin lanterns reflect in Eric's glasses.

'I've been trick or treating,' says Jacob. He's doing something with the tail of his devil costume.

Eric doesn't answer. He pulls back, but Jacob's about twice his size and Eric doesn't get far. 'And I've been eating since I came out of school.' It's hard to see in the dark, but I think Jacob's wrapped the tail of his devil's costume around Eric's hands. 'I've eaten Monster Crunch, chocolate witches, popping candy frogs and toffee.' He lets out a belch. 'Smokey bacon crisps, mint choc chip ice cream, flying saucers, cola, three hot dogs, lemonade, cheesy krispies, sherbert fountains, and chips.' Jacob lets out another belch.

Eric's pressing himself back against the wall, and Jacob's holding him tight. Or rather the mass of Jacob's stomach is holding Eric tight.

'And I had those chips, with loads and loads of brown sauce, and I washed it all down with milk.'

I stare through the dark. I don't think Jacob knows I'm here.

'So all I've got to do is stick my fingers, just like this.'
I see his devil head go back, his fingers against the last
light like a pronged tongue going into his mouth.

'No – you wouldn't.' Eric sounds panicky.

Surely, even Jacob Devlin wouldn't... Maybe he would?
I run five paces further back and before I even think
about it I lift my hand, put the forefinger and thumb
together, and,

Click.

Chapter 12

Oh no. I've really done it now.

Eric's still got his hands tied together, but there's this red string, reaching all the way into my hand. It stops at a little red squirming thing.

A cold hot rush sweeps over me, and for a second I consider dropping it and running.

'Help!' A tiny voice comes from the red shiny grub. Eric walks towards me, and I see that he's gone even whiter, and looks like he's going to be sick again.

'No – it's OK,' I say, although I don't believe it myself for one second. 'I did it.'

'You?' Eric's voice comes out all scratchy and surprised. 'That thing – that's Jacob Devlin?'

I look again at the horrible little grub on my palm, and nod my head.

We sit in Eric's utterly weird bedroom. I think we're both in shock. But Eric's finally stopped shaking. Jacob's shut in a tiny plastic treasure chest. I can hear him squealing. I've got no choice; he has to stay there until he shuts up. Honestly, he's as bad as the donkey. When the shrinking happened he squeaked at me for at least ten minutes, and I had to stick him in my pocket and hold the top shut until we reached Eric's house.

Eric's sitting on the other side of the room. He's back to ordinary snot and white now.

'You, you shrank him?'

I nod.

'Just like that – you, just shrank him?'

I nod again.

'Let me out!' Jacob shouts for the millionth time. We ignore him.

'How?'

'I don't know. I don't understand it. It just happens.'

'It's completely impossible.'

I nod my head.

'No, I mean, it couldn't possibly happen – I mean the laws of physics, biology, everything – it couldn't...'

'It does.'

'Wow,' says Eric.

'Yeah,' I say.

'Wow wow and triple wow,' he says.

I nod.

'Do it again,' he says.

I look around for something that really doesn't matter. There's a huge chocolate bar on the desk, by the laptop. I put my forefinger and thumb together and,

Click.

I turn over my palm, and it's lying there, except now it's only about the size of a dolls' chocolate bar.

Eric stares at it, stares at me, and stares back at it. 'That cost me two quid – look at it now! That's not worth 2p.'

'Sorry,' I say. 'But you wanted me to prove it.'

'Wow,' he says.

'What's going on out there – let me out!'

I pick up the squealing treasure chest. 'Only if you'll be quiet.'

'How do you do it?' asks Eric.

I look into Eric's face. Do I trust him? There's snot and carrot and hairs stuck to his face. All smeared about with white make-up. How could you not trust someone who looks like that?

I pull the meteorite out of my pocket. 'This fell from the sky, right in front me. In the model village.'

Eric turns the meteorite over in his hands, stroking the shiny black bits, and weighing it, just like I did. 'Like a shooting star?'

'Let me out or I'll never talk to you again.'

'Very like a shooting star,' I say.

'And, you wished on it?' says Eric.

'Yes, but my wish didn't have anything to do with shrinking. I don't understand where that came from.'

'I'll kill you, Model Village!'

'Does that mean that if I have the meteorite in my pocket, I can shrink things?'

I shrug. 'Try.' I hand him the meteorite. 'Put your middle finger and your thumb together, make a little circle, hold your hand about six inches in front of your eye, and click in your head, as if it was a camera.'

Eric's concentrating really hard. He's got his fingers in a circle and he's staring at a shoe lying on the other side of the room.

'Let me out!'

Eric lets his breath out in a big rush. He shakes his head. 'No…it just works for you. It must be because you were the first to touch it, or something. But, wow, Tom. Wow.' He turns the meteorite over in his hand. 'Can you make things big again?'

I shake my head.

We both look at the chest. We're both thinking the same thing. Jacob Devlin could be tiny for the rest of his life. Is that such a bad thing? The chest's shaking. It looks really weird. In fact it's all really weird, and now I'm feeling sick too.

'LET ME OUT!'

I pick up the chest. I can feel his weight inside. Almost nothing. 'OK, Jacob,' I say. 'I'm going to open the lid, but you've got to shut up. If you keep shouting, I'll squash you.'

There's a pause, and then he says, 'OK.'

I open it. And there he is, standing there. The little toasting fork in his hand. About two inches high. A raspberry, all in tight-fitting segments, with horns, and a huge tail.

'I'll get you, Model Village. I'll kill you for this.'

I can't help wondering how. He's only two inches tall and I'm four foot six.

'I don't think so,' I say, and flinch, because I'm sort of expecting him to suddenly be big again. But he stays tiny and shakes his toasting fork at me.

'I'll tell my mum, I'll tell my dad – and then you'll be for it, Model Village. You'll be in serious trouble.' He sneers at Eric. 'And you, Snot Face, Four

Eyes, Geek. I'll tell them about this room, won't just be your dad they all laugh at then.' He shakes his tiny fist and stamps his foot.

I look around at the room. Jacob's right, it would be bad if this got out. Probably the least embarrassing thing is a framed picture of Eric; dressed as a fairy.

'Presents from my aunt. She still thinks I'm three,' says Eric, calmly. 'I expect there are some advantages in being small, Jacob. For example, look how big this sweet is now.' Eric rootles about in his trick or treat bag and hands Jacob a jelly baby.

Jacob stops shouting and stares at it. It's only a bit smaller than him; in fact his arms don't quite reach round it. He sticks one finger out, and it sinks into the soft sugar dusting.

'Oh woah – I've died and gone to heaven,' he says, burying his head in the side of the jelly baby.

'Wish I had a camera,' says Eric.

I did this. I DID THIS! But it doesn't make me feel good. 1% good? Maybe 2% good, but not as good as I should feel. The awful thing is, that this shrinking business is not as good as it should be. It's one thing to shrink random things, but people? Planets?

'Um, do you have the internet, Eric? Could you look up – the news? BBC or something.'

'Why?' Then Eric stares at me. 'This doesn't have anything to do with…?'

And I say it. I say it for the first time. I have to close my eyes while I say it – I don't want to see what Eric thinks. 'I shrank Jupiter, and lost it.'

Eric draws in his breath. Jacob does a tiny high-pitched belch.

'You can't have done.'

'I did – I was playing around, and…'

'That's impossible.'

'It happened.'

'Whoops,' says Jacob.

Chapter 13

The sky's really gone off on one now, with shooting stars cascading all around us. People have come out from their houses and are staring up. It's like a huge free firework party. It would be really beautiful if it wasn't so terrifying.

Eric points up at the sky. 'See – see what you've done? This is even worse than they predicted...'

'Nit,' shouts Jacob, from my pocket.

I feel 1000% rubbish now.

'It's your fault, Jacob,' I point out. 'If you didn't go round stealing things off people then I'd still have Jupiter in my pocket and we'd be able to try and stick it back in the sky. It's your fault the planet's ended up ground into the gravel.'

'S'cuse me, Model Village, if you didn't go round shrinking things then none of this would have happened.'

We're walking back to school. Eric seemed to think that all we really needed to do was to find Jupiter, dead or alive – that once it was back in the sky, all this would stop.

'Back in the sky?' I asked. 'How?'

'I'm sure there's a way,' said Eric.

I suggested that as Jacob was so small, it might be easy for him to find the planet.

'Naff off!' he said.

But then I pointed out that he was two inches tall, and that my feet were quite big, compared to his head.

Eric's dad passes us. He's leaving cables along the side of the road.

'Why?' I ask Eric.

'It's complicated,' says Eric.

I look up at the sky now. Just in case Jupiter's back where it should be.

'Thing is, though,' says Eric, answering a question that no one asked, 'it takes around forty-three minutes for us to see what's up there.'

'What?

'Light years – it takes that long for the image of an object the distance of Jupiter, to appear to us on Earth.'

'How do you know this stuff?' I ask.

'He's a nerd,' says Jacob. We both ignore him.

Eric shrugs. 'I also know that Jupiter takes about twelve years to orbit the sun, that it's more than seven hundred and seventy million miles from the sun, that the red spot's really a storm that's been raging for more than three hundred years. That it has a moon called Io. I could go on.'

'Don't,' says Jacob.

'Who's that?' says Eric, pointing towards Grandma's house.

I've sort of forgotten about 'Mr and Mrs Magic's Night of Halloween Fun', so when Mum and Dad and Tilly blunder out into the street light in front of us, I'm not prepared.

The pumpkins are Mum and Tilly – Dad's dressed as Dracula. He's got wonky stick-on teeth, and his hair's dyed black. He's wearing his 'I drink blood for breakfast' braces. He's waving his arms at us. He actually looks completely mad.

'Whooooo, whooooo, whooo – anyone ready for a little nibble?' he says in this stupid voice. 'Are you coming to watch an evening of hilarious, heart-rending, horrifying, humungous, hair-raising, Halloween Magic!'

'Oh, Daddy and Daddy – can't we go?' shouts Jacob from my pocket.

Mum stares at me and I start imaginary coughing.

'Um,' says Eric.

'No,' I whisper.

'No,' says Eric, and we run, legging it down the street until we reach the model village, and pause in the dark for Eric to breathe. It's so warm I'm sweating.

'If my parents were as pants as that – I'd emigrate,' says Jacob.

I think of Jacob's pink round mother and boring head-master father. 'If I had parents like yours I'd emigrate.'

'What's wrong with my parents?' he says.

'What's wrong with mine?' I reply.

'Yours must be soooooooo embarrassing.'

'Yours too.'

'All parents are embarrassing,' says Eric. 'Even grand-parents are embarrassing. That's what they're there for. Come on, let's try running again.'

Chapter 14

We race past the model village. Tilly's left a pumpkin lantern on the wall.

'Hey, that reminds me.' I leap over the wall. 'I've got these things I shrank earlier.'

'I want to see – let me down!'

I'd like to call him Snot Face Four Eyes, but the best I can think of is 'Squit'. 'OK, Squit,' I say, and open the flap at the top of my pocket. He climbs out on to the ground. Yuk, he still looks really weird.

I chuck my backpack down and reach into it for my tiny prizes.

Eric clangs the gate. 'Woah – what are these?' He picks up the tiny bench and admires it. 'Hey – that's from the seafront... I know that – it's got my name on it. My aunt paid for it, when I was born.'

'My aunt paid for it, when I was born. Bless. When I was born, my dad got a row of seats at Bywater Regis Football Club. And he paid for them, they cost thousands. They've all got my name on.'

'That's nice,' says Eric, and he says it as if he means it.

Eric helps me balance the pumpkins on the miniature windowsills. He takes the candle out of Tilly's big pumpkin on the wall and Jacob relights all the small ones.

They glow like a line of orange berries.

I put the bench in front. And the plastic hot dog alongside. I wonder if Grandma'll notice.

'They look brilliant,' says Eric.

Jacob tries sitting on the bench. 'It's a bit big,' he says.

I'm just about to pick up the bench when I hear something.

Tap, clunk. Tap, clunk.

Grandma?

She appears from out of the darkness behind us. She's not dressed up, but she's got the plastic bag on her head again. I know she's round and cosy to look at, but she's still scary, especially coming out of the dark like that.

I grab Jacob and stuff him in my trouser pocket. He's wriggling.

'Hello! Granny!' he shouts.

I go into another fit of imaginary coughing.

'Hello, boys. What are you up to?'

'Nothing,' I say.

'Watching the shooting stars,' says Eric, pointing at the sky.

'Hmm,' she says, in that way grown-ups say when they don't believe you. 'It's a very unhappy solar system – with Jupiter missing.' She stares at me. I look at the ground. 'Nice lanterns you've got there. Have you seen mine? Take a look at the bowls club as you pass.' She moves off towards the house. 'There's some oxtail soup for you, Tom, on the stove, when you're peckish.'

'Bye,' I say, watching her sink back into the darkness, and waiting until I see the yellow square of the door open and close around her. 'Phew.' I open my hand so that Jacob can stand up.

'I nearly told her,' he says, his shiny devil outfit glistening in the shooting starlight.

'I nearly squashed you,' I say.

'You wouldn't,' he says.

'He would,' says Eric. 'Wouldn't you, Tom?'

'I might.'

Jacob goes quiet for a minute. 'Why don't you?'

'Why'd you think?' I say.

'Because he's a scaredy cat?'

'Because he's not a horrible person,' says Eric.

I can almost hear the cogs turning in Jacob's brain.

'I'd squash you if you were tiny.'

'We know,' says Eric. 'But just because you'd squash us, doesn't mean we'd squash you.'

'Does that mean I'm a horrible person?'

We don't bother to reply.

Chapter 15

We run on, but stop at the miniature bowling green. There are four tiny pumpkin lanterns there, and Jacob clambers down to inspect them.

'These are awesome,' he says.

'They can't be as good as mine,' I say.

'Well, they are.'

'But Grandma made them.'

'Your gran's pretty amazing,' says Eric.

Jacob skips off across the bowling green.

'Is she?' I thought Grandma was just scary Grandma.

'Oh yes,' says Eric. 'She's looked after my dad for years, and run this place, making loads of things for it every year, running the cafe and all that stuff. I remember her making me a miniature garden – it was brilliant, real flowers and everything.' Eric waves his arms about as if it was still in front of him. 'I won the village show that year. They gave me a box of jelly fruits.'

'Yuk,' says Jacob. 'I hate jelly fruits, I'd only enter the village show if they had proper prizes.'

'Like what?'

'Like a games console, or a laptop, or hard cash. That stuff's for sissies.'

'It's about taking part,' says Eric. 'Not winning.'

'Why would you want to do that?'

Eric stares at the little red bulbous thing on the ground in front of him. 'If you don't get it, then I can't possibly explain.'

I pick up one of Grandma's pumpkins. It's completely perfect.

'Grandma sent us here on purpose,' I say. 'She's suspicious about the meteorite, and she wanted me to see that her pumpkins were as good as mine.'

'Why?' asks Eric.

'Exactly,' I answer.

We move on through the model village, the meteor showers now filling the whole sky, except for one small cloud hanging over the sea.

'Wow,' says Jacob, climbing into the miniature post office window. 'I didn't realise how pants these buildings were. They're really rubbish.'

'Thanks, I think I knew that.'

'They're all junk, except this one.' He stops by a barn that I've never noticed before. 'This,' he says, 'is not pants. Look, it's even got those mushroom things underneath. And, woah, there's tiny initials scratched in the stone. Did your gran make this? Awesome.'

I shine my torch at the barn. It's not in the real village – so why's it in the model village?

'Hey – and this – this is mega.' He's standing next to a water trough. 'It's even got the writing on it – 1888, presented by, oh, I dunno, some boring bloke. Awesome.'

Lit by fairy lights in the trees, Jacob chases off through the houses.

Eric's stopped. He's staring at the barn. 'I've seen photos of this. This used to be in the real village. It was taken by aliens, just when Dad was abducted. A whole load of things went, all at the same time. There's a newspaper cutting about it, on the stairs, at home.'

'You mean this *was* in the village, and then disappeared?'

'Yeah. Although why would the aliens shrink it and leave it here? I don't know.'

Luckily, in the dark, Eric can't see the colour of my face. I feel the flush charge down my back and right down to my feet. So it's happened before. There must be someone else who's done this, someone who hid the things in the model village. But they can't have done Eric's dad, otherwise he'd still be tiny. That really must have been aliens. I stand staring at Jacob's shiny red body skipping through the model village.

My brain grinds into action.

'How old is your dad?'

'Why?'

'Just how old is he?'

'Fifty-five.'

Fifty-five years ago. Grandma would have been here then, Grandma's always been here. It was her father's house before. He started the model village and she grew up in my bedroom.

I glance back at the perfect pumpkin lanterns on the bowling green.

'Eric, it's Grandma!'

'Grandma?'

'She must know. She's the one. That's why she's been following me, looking in my bag. That's why she wanted me to see the pumpkins.'

'What do you mean?' Eric stops. 'You think she can shrink things too?'

'The night that the meteorite fell,' I say. 'She didn't want me to get it. She didn't want me to wish.'

'Because she can do it herself?'

Chapter 16

I stand paralysed.

Eric grabs me by the arm. 'Come on,' he says. 'We'd better get a move on. We need to find Jupiter as soon as possible.'

'But, Eric – even if we find it, I don't know how to put it back.'

'Ask your grandma. If she can shrink things – she can probably unshrink them.'

Ask Grandma? A shudder of fear runs down my neck. 'Bet she can't,' I say. 'I can't, can I?'

'Bet she can. Your grandma can do most things.'

Jacob clambers over Eric's shoe and undoes one of his shoelaces.

'But what if we can't find it?' I think of another excuse.

'We won't know, if we don't look,' says Eric, sounding a lot like Grandma.

'But, but...'

'What is it?

'I can't ask her,' I whisper. 'I'm too scared.'

'Oh! We're all going to die. Model Village has messed up the solar system. We're going to crash into the sun and fry – if we're not squashed by a giant asteroid first, and all because scaredy Model Village doesn't want to ask scary granny.'

'Oh, do shut up, Jacob,' Eric says. 'Anyway, I've been thinking, if Jupiter's about 143,000 kilometres in diameter, and it has a magnetic field of 1,600,000 kilometres, then even if it's only the size of a bead, it would still have a magnetic field – it would have a pull.'

'What?'

'How big was Jupiter?'

'What are you on about?'

Jacob undoes Eric's other shoelace.

'How big was Jupiter – before you lost it?' He says 'lost' like I did it on purpose.

'Half a centimetre, maybe.'

Eric mutters to himself and stares at his fingers. 'One million six hundred thousand, one hundred and sixty thousand, sixteen thousand, take the noughts off – then that's divided by a hundred and forty-six thousand, so, take away the zeros all round – um, about five centimetres. It would have a magnetic pull of five centimetres.'

'Five centimetres?'

He nods. His glasses reflect the fairy lights but I can't see what he's thinking.

'We can't exactly drop a nail and watch Jupiter suck it towards it, can we? I mean, you've got to be pretty close already to notice a magnetic pull of five centimetres. That's about the size of a saucer.'

Eric nods, his face creasing with disappointment. He removes Jacob from his shoe; gently pulling the laces from Jacob's tiny hands, and placing him back on the ground.

'Still,' I say. 'It was a good idea. Let's get to school. I'm sure you're right about the magnetic thing. Anything that helps us find it...'

I wish Eric *was* right. And I wish I had the courage to tell Grandma. I'm starting to feel so sick about this that I'd like to go back to her house and climb under the duvet with a comic, and stay there for a week.

Perhaps I'll wake up on my birthday and find it was all a horrible dream.

Jacob puts his hands up to be carried like a fat red baby. Eric's already down by the crazy golf, so I have to pick Jacob up. He sits on my shoulder.

'Gee up, horsy, this is fun!'

I don't deliberately give Jacob a bumpy ride, but I'm not as careful as I should be and he quickly clambers down to sit in the crook of my arm.

'Got any sweets?'

'No.'

'No toffee squashed in the bottom of your pocket?'

'The only thing I want to find squashed at the bottom of my pocket is you, Squit.'

No one cares about us as we run along the seafront. They're all staring at the sky. We stop at the side of the castle. We can cut ten minutes off the walk if we go through the castle grounds.

'It's a bit spooky...' says Eric.

Inside, I agree, but I'm not going to confess in front of Jacob. 'I don't think so – come on.'

I climb over the railings and run straight ahead into the darkness. Eric thumps along behind me.

'Whoooooooooo, whoooooooooo,' calls Jacob from my shoulder.

'I could just leave you here,' I say. 'On your own, in the dark.'

'You wouldn't.'

'You never know,' says Eric. And then we're out the other side and the school's in front of us.

Chapter 17

The playground's weird at night, really unfriendly. A cat looms up out of the dark and Eric jumps.

'Whoooooo!' says Jacob, so I drop him in the sandpit.

'But you need me!' he shouts. I let him lie there for a moment, then, really slowly, I pick him up.

'I'd have left you there,' he says, clambering up to my elbow.

'Would you really?' asks Eric.

Jacob doesn't answer.

We stop where the fight happened. Eric holds the torch and I put Jacob down on the ground. He sets off along the beam of the torch, and then stops.

'Nah, it's no good, I need to hold the torch, get the angle right.'

Eric lays the torch on the ground and Jacob rolls it round in a big circle. 'Bingo!'

'What? Can you see it?' asks Eric.

'No. But it's fun. Bet I'm having more fun than you two, Scaredy Four Eyes, and Scaredy Model Village.'

I could just squash him.

I stare at the ground just in case I can see anything. Glistening, red and fat, like a pair of tiny Edam cheeses, Jacob bounces among the lumps of gravel in and out of the torchlight. He stops and walks towards something. 'Oh – it's nothing, just a broken bead. Sorreeee.'

'Where?'

'Over here. But it's not Jupiter.'

Jacob's standing next to something exactly the same colour as the rest of the gravel. I pick it up. It's half a brown bead. A dull wooden bead. I close my eyes and try to remember how Jupiter looked the last time I looked inside the capsule. It looked very like this.

'Look – here's the other half.' Jacob's standing at the very edge of the torchlight and I can't even see what he's pointing at. He moves it, and I pick it up. It's the missing piece.

'Coo, so Model Village can put two bits of bead together. He's a genius. Pity he's going to kill us all – by messing about with things he doesn't understand.'

I really could just step on him, but he's lucky because my mind's turning over again. It's turning over and over on these bits of bead. The other two are still searching for

Jupiter, but I don't think it's there – I think this is the Jupiter that I took to school, and that it wasn't Jupiter at all. Somehow, I lost it in my bedroom, and this lousy bead must have been in the capsule all along.

Jupiter must have rolled out when the capsule was lying on the floor. I must have kicked it somewhere.

'C'mon, Tom,' says Eric.

'Yes,' I say in answer, but I don't really mean it. If this bead was the dead planet in the bottom of the capsule, then perhaps the planet isn't dead. Perhaps somewhere in Grandma's house, there's a little glitter ball going round and round.

Maybe Jupiter's back in my bedroom after all.

Chapter 18

I turn to run back to the house.

'Hey, Tom, where are you going?!' shouts Eric.

But I can't stop. 'I don't think it's here – I think it's at Grandma's.'

'What?' Eric says. 'What are we doing here, then?'

'Too difficult to explain. C'mon – no time to waste.'

I pick up Jacob and stick him on my shoulder. 'Yeth, come on, Tom, save the planet.'

Eric doesn't say anything, just sighs and heads back towards the castle.

I follow him. It doesn't take me long to catch up, and we walk next to each other over the edge of the rock that the castle's built on. It's not spooky any more, the sky's bright, and the castle grounds are all lit up. The big rock almost glows in the starlight. I stop for a moment and stare. It's like it's reflecting more than the meteor showers. It's as if it's got a star inside.

'Weird,' says Jacob.

'It's always been like that,' says Eric. 'Dad says the castle's built on a giant meteorite, one that fell millions of years ago. That's why this is such a special place. The whole town's full of special people too.' He prods me. 'You're one of them now.'

'How d'you mean? Special.'

'You can do things, weird things. There's Miss Darling, for a start.'

'Who?'

'The one who always wears gloves?'

'What can she do?'

'She's got green fingers.'

'Yuk,' says Jacob.

'What d'you mean, green?' I ask.

'I mean, she's actually got green fingers. Like an alien, but it makes her plants grow really well.'

'Er-ic,' says Jacob. 'I've never heard such rubbish.'

'Well, it's true. Ask your gran, Tom.'

This is all news to me.

'Do you think your dad's a special person, with special powers?' I ask.

Eric stumbles off ahead. 'Nah — Dad was definitely taken by aliens, otherwise how else would you explain him?'

I follow, my feet slipping on the glittering rock.

Chapter 19

We run back along the seafront to Grandma's. The air's warm on my face, I could really enjoy this if I didn't feel the weight of chaos on my shoulders.

And Jacob.

'Are we going back to yours then, Model Village? Or are you going to take me home, explain me to my mum and dad? Oh – sorry, Mr and Mrs Devlin, I accidentally on purpose shrank your little cherub.'

Jacob seems heavier. It might just be that he's becoming more of a pain. Eric said that no matter how daffy his dad was, there was no way he'd miss a tiny devil living in the house. So I'm landed with him.

'I'll put you in the model village. You can have your own house.'

'I'm not living there. It's stinky and gross. I want a warm

room, with comfy chairs, beds and stuff, and plenty of food.'

'How about Tilly's dolls' house?'

'How about your bedroom?'

We stop to stare at a house in the high street. A load of people are trying to get a dinghy out of the front door. They've taken down the mast, but it doesn't want to fit.

They joggle it backwards and forwards, and a little bit sideways. It's really stuck.

'Weird,' says Jacob. 'That's my friend's house. I didn't know he had a boat.'

'How did they ever get it in?' I ask.

A man takes the front door off its hinges. The dinghy scrapes out on to the front path.

It's funny how everyone paints boats the same colours, blue and white. It's just like the one I shrank in the bay, only smaller – or maybe bigger?

Chapter 20

The telly's on really loud, so we sneak in without Grandma noticing, and find my bedroom smells like a farmyard. It sounds like one too.

'MOOO.'

'EEYORE.'

'BAAA.'

Oh no – they've changed. They're much bigger than I remember, more like blueberry muffins than popcorn, and they've pooed *all* over the carpet. They've also eaten every scrap of grass and they've chewed a hole in my duvet cover. I didn't know sheep grew that fast. Perhaps they were lambs?

Whoops.

'Wow!' says Eric.

'Woah!' says Jacob. 'Now that's weird. What you got them in

your bedroom for, Model Village? Shouldn't they be outside, running around in the mini haystacks?'

'It's not like you, worrying about something else,' says Eric.

'What d'you mean – not like me? Anyway – I don't like cruelty to animals,' says Jacob, rubbing one of the sheep between the ears.

'But,' Eric says, 'you don't care about cruelty to people?'

'I'm not cruel. That's just mucking about.'

'Hmmm,' says Eric.

'Quick, while Grandma's watching the news, let's stick them in the model village,' I say to Eric.

I bundle the donkey and the cows into a plastic policeman's helmet, and Eric picks up the cardboard box full of sheep.

'Am I coming?'

'No, you stay here,' I say, 'and look for Jupiter.'

Jacob looks at the room. 'Where's the telly, then?'

'Downstairs. Anyway, you don't need it, you're looking for a planet.'

'What – no TV? What d'you play your games on, then?'

I shake my head. 'No telly, no games console, no laptop. There's Dad's catch-the-baby-from-the-burning-building thing, but Tilly's got the games. Otherwise, the radio. You'll have to read a book, Jacob.'

'Or look for Jupiter,' says Eric.

'Got any comics?'

I put the radio on, and we leave Jacob on the floor, measuring himself against the cartoons, and tiptoe downstairs.

Outside in the model village, we let the little animals free. They mix in with Grandma's lumpy resin sheep. Mine are a bit smaller, but they look fantastic skipping through the tiny houses.

'Seems a shame to let them go, really,' says Eric.

We're caught in a square of yellow light that spills across the grass. I jump, dropping the policeman's helmet. 'On your way home, Eric?' asks Grandma, from the doorway. 'Your dad rang – he's cooking.' She holds the gate open for him.

'Baaaaa.'

'Oh – um, yes, I suppose I was, Mrs Perks,' he says, raising his eyebrows.

I pretend I can't hear the sheep.

The gate squeaks as he opens it. Eric sort of hesitates on the threshold, but Grandma waves him away.

'Go on, dear – home now,' she says.

'Baaaaa.'

Eric waves and heads off along the road to his house.

'Mooo.'

She doesn't even blink. 'Now, Tom – something on your mind?'

I could ask her: can you shrink things? But I daren't. I could ask her: how do you put things back? But I'm too scared. Perhaps there's a way of getting her to tell me what I want to know, without me telling her what she wants to know.

'Why didn't you want me to wish?' I ask.

'Didn't I, dear? When was that?'

A tiny sheep wanders out from the model village. It's standing by the church, looking up at Grandma, like she's a really big bit of grass.

'Baaaa.'

Oh no. I'll have to take emergency action. 'No, Grandma, you didn't – and you didn't want me to find this.'

I take the meteorite out of my pocket and Grandma's eyes widen. I walk back towards the front door, so that she's looking towards me, and not towards the sheep.

'Did you wish?' she says.

'No,' I lie, 'but what would have happened if I had?'

She doesn't say anything for a minute, just follows me up the step and into the house.

'Moooo.'

Chapter 21

'In this village, Tom, dear – you have to be careful what you wish for. When I was a little girl I wished on a shooting star.'

'Did you?'

Grandma's spooning oxtail soup into a mug. There's a big ladle hanging on the wall, but she's using a little one. Grandma's always using things that are the wrong size.

The soup's kind of purple and sticky. I hope she's not thinking of giving it to me. I take an apple from the sideboard. It's huge, but delicious.

'Yes – I wished something silly, really.' She's filling another mug now.

'What did you wish for?'

She ignores my question. 'The meteorite landed in our

garden, just like the one you've got there, and I picked it up, just as you did. It was by the castle.'

'Here – this castle? In the model village?'

Grandma nods. 'They say the real castle's built on a giant piece of space rock, one that fell millions of years ago. This was just a small one. Perfect, really. It fitted in the palm of my hand.'

'And you saw it fall?'

She nods. 'Just like that one you've got there. It banged, as it came down – a real thunderclap – and then whacked into the lavender, right in front of me.'

She carves a chunk of her homemade bread, and crashes it into a battered old tray as if it was the meteorite.

'The thing is, after that – I found I could shrink things.' She stares really hard at me, and I nearly choke on the apple.

'Shrink? How – extraordinary.'

'Hmm.' She bangs one of the mugs of soup on to the tray and reaches into a drawer in the dresser. 'Here you are.'

She pulls out a cloth bundle and unwraps it on the table. A small, ordinary, smoothed stone rolls out from a bundle of ancient, crumbling lavender.

'Woah, Grandma.' I pick it from her hand. It's very

heavy, just like mine. So I put them side by side on the kitchen table. We both stare. They're about the same colour and size. Both are odd shapes.

'They could come from the same rock,' she says, stroking mine with her cracked old fingers. 'Extraordinary, extraordinary.'

'What's extraordinary?' I ask.

'The cosmos, dear. It's quite extraordinary, for example, that the night your meteorite fell, Jupiter vanished.'

'Is it?' I say weakly.

'Yes – you wouldn't know anything about it, I suppose?'

Chapter 22

Did you know that stick-on Dracula teeth look exactly like plastic dinosaur claws?

I know that, because Mum and Dad and Tilly save me from Death By Grandma by bursting back into the kitchen, and Dad's false teeth shoot out of his mouth all over the floor.

Mum scrabbles about picking them up and it turns out that one of them is a plastic dinosaur claw.

Grandma stuffs her meteorite back in the drawer. I stick mine in my pocket. She snaps me a look that says the subject won't be forgotten, that she'll be asking again before the evening's out.

'How did it go?' asks Grandma.

'Fabulous – fantastic – they loved us.'

'And did the disappearing cupboard work?'

Mum and Dad look at each other.

'Not exactly,' says Mum.

'It was really funny,' says Tilly. 'Mum lost Dad, and the rabbits got stuck in the middle, and ran out all over the stage. The audience couldn't stop laughing, they thought it was on purpose.'

'So did you enjoy it?' I ask.

'Have a good fight?' she asks, without even looking at me.

'Have a good time dressed as a pumpkin?'

'You must be really stupid choosing Jacob Devlin.'

'Thanks. Do you know where the games for Dad's catch-the-baby-from-the-burning-building thing are?'

'They're not in my room and you can't go and look for them.'

'I'll be careful.'

'No – and I'll know if you've been in there, and I'll kill you if you have. Anyway, they're not there.'

'If they're not there, why would I go in and look for them.'

'Exactly.'

Most of the time, I don't understand Tilly.

Carrying a mug of oxtail goo, I escape upstairs, only to find Jacob and the squirrel standing nose to nose on either side of an empty cereal bowl. Oddly, they're almost exactly the same height, and probably, the same weight. The squirrel's tail is all fluffed up. It looks really angry.

They're circling round the bowl, first to the left, then back to the right.

The squirrel's got evil-looking claws, and with its lips pulled back, a nasty sharp-toothed scowl.

Jacob's holding his toasting fork, but I don't think much of his chances against the squirrel.

'Stay st—' I shout, but Jacob jumps on the side of the bowl, flicking the other side up and cracking the squirrel on the underside of his jaw.

The squirrel yelps and leaps back into the corner. I throw myself forward to catch it, but it hides in a pile of socks. Jacob stands and brushes his hands together. 'See – no problem – I can deal with anything. I'm a genius, see? Have you got the games?'

'As you're a genius, have you found Jupiter?'

Jacob slaps himself on the forehead. 'Oh – I forgot to tell you... It was in the... Of course not, you idiot. Anyway, they've told us all about it on the radio. It seems that we're most likely to be spattered with asteroids and comets before catapulting into the sun and roasting. Oh, and the Taj Mahal's been destroyed, and the Arizona desert now looks like Eric's skin and worst of all, a huge piece of rock has broken off from the Asteroid Belt and is on a collision course with Earth.'

'Oh.'

'And it's due to hit Earth the day after tomorrow, 2nd November.' Jacob sounds quite pleased. As if he doesn't really live on Earth.

'That's my birthday.'

'Sorreee.'

I now feel completely sick. I really would like to go to bed until my birthday, and I'd like someone else to sort this whole thing out. And I'd like Jacob to go away.

We've spent an hour searching the floor for Jupiter, or at least I have. Jacob's been slurping oxtail soup and singing Queen's back catalogue in a squeaky helium voice.

He's got the top of the little games console open, and he's catching babies. It looks like a widescreen TV next to him.

'Still no games?' he says, just like Tilly would.

'I'm going for a wee,' I say.

'What about the squirrel?'

I look around the bedroom for a secure place to put Jacob. I spot a blob of chewing gum that I stuck to the mirror last week. 'Here – this'll keep you safe.' I take it, stick it in my mouth and chew until it goes soft and stick it to his back. Then I press him to the wall over the wash-basin.

I *do* put the plug in.

'Hey! You can't leave me like this!' But I can, and I turn on the radio, really loudly, and slip out of the door.

Chapter 23

I can't get to sleep. I don't think Jacob can either, although at one point I hear tiny snoring. But I suppose it could be the squirrel. Jacob's on the windowsill by my bed now, sleeping in one of my socks.

I can't stop thinking about Grandma and shrinking. She must have shrunk loads of things. All the Christmas trees in the model village, the tiny gnomes in the tiny crazy golf, the street parties – all of that fiddly stuff must have been her.

And I'd always thought she was just weird.

When I do sleep, I dream that I miss my birthday. That I wake up and the whole day's gone past, and everyone's forgotten about it. Then I dream that Mr and Mrs Magic do a birthday party for me, and invite the whole school, and I go and I'm only wearing my pants and I wake up sweating. I lie awake staring at the meteor showers, and I must fall asleep again because this time I dream of giant asteroids crashing into Australia – I can tell it's Australia because the streets are bounding with koalas and the trees hang with kangaroos.

I get up half a dozen times in the night to look for Jupiter in different places in my room.

The last dream I have before morning is of Grandma, peering into my ears and pulling out my thoughts with a crochet hook. It's really scary. When the alarm goes off, Jacob's sleeping like a baby on my pillow, his face all spattered with Grandma's oxtail soup. He liked it so much he climbed into the mug to lick up the last bits.

Ugh.

Tilly's up early too. She's got music playing in her room and I can hear her dancing.

'She's in there – get the games off her, will you?'

'No – I'm going to look for Jupiter.'

'I'll scream, I'll get Granny.'

I knock on Tilly's door, and try to push it open, but it's barricaded. 'Tilly, have you got the games?'

'Go away.'

'Please.'

'Go away, Tom. You wouldn't play with me, so I'm never, ever going to play with you.'

'But I'm not asking to play with you. I'm asking for a game.'

Silence.

'Tilly?'

More silence.

I go back to my room.

'No luck with the game,' I say.

'You just don't know how to deal with her,' he says.

'You try,' I say.

'Are we going to school?' he asks.

I nod.

'Oh goody. I can tell everyone about my adventures with Uncle Tom and Uncle Eric.'

'No.' I shrink three comics, and a slightly broken cracker toy. I drop them into a camera case, with an apple, a torch and some jelly beans. Jacob should fit down the side, but I have to take out the apple, because he's not as small as I thought. 'You can't tell anyone anything. Jump in, and keep quiet.'

I wonder if you can catch a sheep with a corned beef sandwich?

The animals have moved down into the crazy golf – I can hear them baaing and mooing like mad down there.

It's amazing that Grandma hasn't spotted them. I'll have to do something with them later; they can't live in the model village for ever.

Eric's on the bus. We're all wearing polo shirts, no sweatshirts today, even though it's the first of November. The henchmen sit on the back seat, muttering. Without Jacob they seem smaller.

He's singing in my pocket. 'I want to break free...' No chance. Luckily the grindy gears on the bus drown him out.

I walk into school, staring up at the sky. In the day it's all less frightening – you can't see the meteorites crashing through the atmosphere. It almost feels normal. It's almost normal to have a tiny devil in my pocket. It's almost normal to have lost a planet. It's just very warm.

During registration, everyone's talking about Jacob going missing. The police are here, they want to talk to us all. Apparently, Jacob's been taken by a gang from London and sold into child slavery. Apparently, he's so clever he's been taken by boffins from an American university and wired into their computer.

As if. Why would anyone want Jacob Devlin?

My insides are knotted with worry now. We still haven't

found Jupiter, so I stare out of the window, pretending to be bored, but actually I'm ready to click on an asteroid if it decides to crash here.

The police come into our classroom, they're all sweaty. Three men, three women. I expect they work as a team. Together, they're achieving more.

They break up and start questioning us. There's no getting away from it; they're going to want to speak to us all. Mr Bell takes them round, he looks all serious and mournful.

'The poor little lamb,' he says. Lamb? I'd always seen Jacob as more of a pig.

'Now, lad,' says one particularly tall policeman, bending down to talk to me. He smells of aftershave and bacon sandwiches. 'I'm sure it's distressing, I'm sure it's a worry, but you're not to bother yourself – it won't happen to you.'

I nod. I try to look sorry. I keep my eyes turned down. In my pocket I can feel Jacob jumping up and down inside the camera case. I give him a gentle squeeze to shut him up.

He bites me.

OW! Shivers run up and down my spine and I feel myself start to cry. Ow, that hurt. The policeman takes one look at my face and pulls a chair up. He sort of folds on to it, and puts his head on one side, giving me that 'I understand' look. 'Don't cry, lad, it'll be fine, you'll see.'

I keep my mouth shut and nod my head.

'Thing is, we're wondering if you saw young Jacob last night, out and about? Were you trick or treating?'

I shake my head. Then nod. I can't pretend I wasn't out – Eric might say we were out together. Oh no! What is Eric going to say? I look across, he's talking to a policewoman. He looks as if he's saying quite a lot.

'You were, or you weren't.'

'I was,' I say, as quietly as possible. I need to keep this upset thing going. I sniff, loudly, and the policeman digs in his pocket for a tissue.

'So what time do you think you went out?' asks the policeman.

'About six?' What's Eric going to say?

'And did you see Jacob?'

'I did.' Now why did I say that?

The policeman holds up his hand, and a policewoman appears, looking all concerned. Mr Bell follows – he looks even more concerned.

There's a horrible silence in the classroom, and from deep in my pocket, I hear Jacob yowling like a cat. I put my hand over my stomach and pretend it was me. He's singing something. 'Ring a Ring o' Roses'?

The policemen look at each other and frown.

Too loudly, I say, 'My phone.' No one looks as if they believe me, so I have to start talking to cover the noise. 'Eric was there too. We both saw Jacob – didn't we?'

The girls gasp.

The boys shuffle their feet and bang the chairs.

'Yes,' says Eric, and stares at me.

'He took your sweets – don't you remember?'

The henchmen giggle. The policeman looks round and they shut up, immediately.

'Yes,' says Eric, still staring at me.

'That doesn't sound like Jacob!' says Mr Bell.

The policemen look puzzled.

'It does. He's a bully,' says Eric.

The girls gasp.

'No he's not – he's a gifted and talented youth,' says Mr Bell.

'When was this?' asks the policewoman.

Jacob's yowling again. I can't keep pretending it's my stomach – he's kicking and punching at the camera bag and my hand really hurts.

'Just as it got dark,' I say quickly and loudly. 'We were

near the town hall, he tried to take Eric's sweets, and then I came along and he…'

I can't say, *shrank*.

'Yes?' asks the policewoman.

'Vanished.'

'Yes,' says Eric.

'Where? Vanished?' asks Mr Bell.

'Vanished,' I say.

'Vanished,' says Eric.

Jacob starts singing, 'London's Burning'.

'Into the dark,' I say.

'Into the dark,' says Eric.

'Hmm,' says Mr Bell.

Chapter 24

They finally let us out at lunchtime. By then my stomach really is rumbling. Jacob's bitten through the bag, and is yelling his head off. He's singing rude songs about Eric.

'Dinner hall!' shouts Eric.

Luckily the hall's so noisy no one could possibly hear Jacob, and we take as long as we can to get our packed lunches out of the store.

'Whew,' says Eric.

'Did you hear him?'

'I heard "Twinkle Twinkle Little Star" when Mr Bell was on about strangers and aliens. You should have left him at home.'

'And have Grandma find him?'

Eric sighs. 'What *are* you going to do with him? He can't live like that for ever.'

'He's the least of my worries.'

'I'll come and help you look for Jupiter.'

In the playground, we hide behind the bins and Eric gives Jacob a corner of his tofu sandwich.

Jacob bites into the sandwich and scowls. 'Yuk, Four Eyes, this is disgusting. D'you eat this muck every day?'

'It's nutritious, and healthy. At least I won't die of clogged arteries, and obesity.'

'What d'you mean? Are you calling me obese?'

Eric looks across at me. 'Well, yes,' he says. 'Technically, I think you probably are.'

Jacob squeezes in his gut. It doesn't really get any smaller. But I notice he seems less like a bed bug now, and more like a pile of overripe tomatoes. 'I'm not fat — I'm just, well built.'

'Whatever,' says Eric.

There's a silence while Jacob examines his stomach, rolling it in and out like a Mexican wave.

'So, Model Village, what you going to do? You've been a bit careless with the solar system. Will I be able to tell the world that you're an idiot that messes about with the cosmos? That you, single-handedly, destroyed the Eiffel Tower?'

'You won't be able to tell them anything,' I say, 'from my pocket.'

'They're looking for me.'

'They are,' says Eric.

'You'd get in so much trouble if they found out what's really happened.'

'The size you are now, they'd probably just swat you – think you were a giant ladybird or something.' I smile. 'Or a bird might carry you off. You need us, you know.'

'Yes,' says Eric. 'Without us to explain just what's happened, someone with eyesight like Tom's grandma would think you were a mouse. If you start running around and squealing on the floor – well, who knows…?'

Jacob's tiny face wrinkles up, as if he's just realised what's going on.

'But I could tell them afterwards, when I'm big.'

'You could,' I say. I can't think of a reason why he couldn't. Except that he might never be big again.

'Hmmm, you could – but I wouldn't have believed it if I hadn't seen it happen, right in front of me.' Eric shrugs. 'So go ahead,' he says. 'But they'll think you're mad – like my dad. The only person who ever believed him about the aliens was Tom's grandma. No one else did, not even my mum, not even his mum. He's had years of ridicule. Look at him now.'

'Do you believe him?' I ask.

'Probably. Something massive happened to him.' I can't tell what Eric thinks as he says this – the light shines off his glasses. He points at Jacob. 'A bit like you, really.'

We both stare at Jacob. His face is all crumpled. He's smaller – well, he's not smaller, he's just stopped being big and full.

'I promise.'

'What?'

'I promise to keep quiet. At least I promise to keep quiet while I'm small.'

'Why?'

'Because.'

'Because why?'

'Because I just do.'

Chapter 25

I charge into the house and pound up the stairs, but Grandma's sitting out on the landing, knitting a tiny tent.

'Hello, Tom, love.'

I push Jacob deeper into my pocket.

'Hello, Grandma.'

I dodge for my room.

There's a game lying on the floor outside. Tilly must have left it.

'Tom – is there anything you want to tell me?'

I wish she'd stop asking that.

'N-no.'

I crash in through the door, throwing the game on the bed.

Jacob leaps out of my pocket and runs for the

catch-the-baby thing. He seems bigger now. How did he ever fit in that treasure chest?

'Aren't you going to help?' I whisper, just in case Grandma's listening at the door.

He stares at me for a moment. 'But I always play computer games when I get home from school.'

'Shhh.' I turn on the radio. 'Well, this isn't home. It's a crisis and you gotta help,' I say, dropping to my hands and knees and looking under the chest of drawers for the millionth time.

He takes a long look at the game, opens and closes the lid, then clambers off the table and, much to my surprise, crawls off under the bed. 'Better be a reward, Model Village. Yuk – what's this?' He kicks a cheese and pickle sandwich out from under the bed that I hid from Grandma the first weekend we were here. I was too scared to tell her that I don't like pickle.

I shake each of my shoes out on to a piece of paper. All I find is a teddy bear head and a ten cent coin.

I sit back against the bed and think.

Where else could it be?

Jacob's trying out a toy car, but he won't fit through the window.

I stare at the wall.

There's a drawing pin, stuck to the plaster the wrong way round. The pin seems to be sticking towards me.

Weird.

I get up to have a look and pull at the drawing pin. It comes away quite easily, but when I let go, it sticks to the wall again. Two paper clips and a picture nail hover just above the skirting board. They're not apparently held up by anything.

I pull at them and it feels like pulling a nail away from a magnet.

Magnet?

What did Eric say about magnetic pull? With Jupiter the size it was when it came out of the sky, the magnetic force field would only have been about five centimetres. But the paper clip and the drawing pin are a metre apart. Eric must have got the calculation wrong. The magnetic field must be at least a metre, and it's on the other side of the wall.

Tilly's room.

She's got Jupiter. That's why she won't let me in her room.

Yeah! That means I haven't lost it.

Yippee! Yippee! Yippee! We won't all be fried by the sun, or blasted by asteroids. I've saved the world – I'm a hero.

Except that it's in Tilly's room, she's doing after-school ballet, and Grandma's out there fiddling about.

And I'm still too scared of Grandma.

I pull the door open, really quietly.

I don't breathe. I reckon Grandma can hear breathing. She can't hear the telly but she can hear someone eating a biscuit.

I stick my head out to have a look.

She's still there, really close. There's no way I can get into Tilly's room without her spotting me.

Blast.

So I come back in. Jacob's legs are sticking out from under the bed.

How can I get into Tilly's room? It's only on the other side of the wall. The other side of a five-hundred-year-old stone wall, with no convenient hole in it.

Why is none of this easy?

I check the landing again and Grandma's still there.

Is there any other way in? We could distract her somehow and rush in, but I don't think she's that deaf. Anyway there's always the chance that she would think that Jacob really was a bed bug and squash him.

I look around my bedroom again.

The window.

It's a big sash window, and it nearly fully opens. I push it up as far as it'll go. It wedges open.

I stick my head out and look along the front of the house to Tilly's room. There's a ledge that runs along under the windows, but I don't think you're supposed to walk along it, and below is the model village church with a tall spire.

Ow.

'BAAA.'

Over by the miniature bowling green I can see the sheep, and they're looking enormous. In fact they're looking almost full-sized.

Are they growing?

I stare at them for a second longer. No – that's impossible.

Shame there aren't any underneath the window, they'd make a nice soft landing pad.

I look back inside.

'Jacob?' I say nicely.

'Hm?' His mouth is jammed with something green and sticky. A forgotten jelly baby?

'How are you on heights?'

'Can't do them. Sorry, mate.' He smiles at me.

'Not even to save the planet?'

He shakes his head and crawls off under the bed. Interesting – he didn't call me 'Model Village'.

I sit on the windowsill and swing my legs over. They dangle in space. This is not a nice feeling. It's like sitting on the top board at the swimming pool, but instead of water there's crazy paving. I look up instead of down. It's nearly dark now and the meteor showers have got going again. Another firework display.

If Eric was here he'd tell me that the meteor showers were getting more frequent, or closer or something. But I don't want to know. I just want to get Jupiter back, and get it up in the sky.

My feet settle on the ledge. I swing round so that I've got my back to the world, my toes on the ledge, and I'm facing the wall.

Then I creep along. One step. Another step, a third, and I can feel the opening for Tilly's window.

Whew.

I take one more pace and I'm right there. The curtains are drawn – there's nothing to see. I slip my fingers under the edge of the sash and pull.

Nothing happens.

'BAAAA.'

I pull again.

Nothing happens again.

I peer in. Nothing's going to happen. She's put the window lock across.

No.

I slip my fingers under the edge – perhaps I can slide the lock over. But it's too stiff and stays just as it is.

I look back at my window, just in time to see it slide shut.

CRASH.

NO!

DON'T PANIC.

'EEYORE.'

I swallow. I won't panic. Instead, I'll stretch my leg as far as it will go, and I'll edge back along the ledge until I'm standing on the sill.

Then, I'm sure there'll be a way in.

'EEYORE.'

But when I get to my window, Jacob's on the inside, looking surprised. He bends down as if he could push up the sash, but there's no chance, he's too tiny. I try pushing too, but it won't move – there's nothing to hold on to out here.

Oh no. This cannot be real.

I scrabble with my nails against the wood, but the paint just flakes off in my hands.

'MOOOOO.' I glance down. Below me, a cow plucks a tea towel from the washing line.

I stare at Jacob through the glass.

He's got this Jacob grin on his face. I can't hear him, but he's saying something, and now he's laughing.

'Jacob!' I say. 'Do something.'

But all he does is jump up and down on the window-sill, pointing and laughing.

And then I see something behind him. Something's moving in the shadows.

It's the squirrel.

'Jacob – the squirrel.'

He shakes his head and goes on laughing.

But it is the squirrel; it's coming up behind him. Frantically, I tap on the window. 'Squirrel!' I bellow. 'Squirrel – behind you!!!'

Jacob rolls theatrically on the windowsill.

The squirrel seems bigger now – much bigger than Jacob. Like a T-Rex hanging over a short, fat Father Christmas.

I hammer on the window. 'Jacob, you nit! It's right there.'

Jacob turns and sees the squirrel. His eyebrows disappear inside the hood of his devil costume and he claws at the inside of the window.

The squirrel lunges forward.

No!

And then, just as I'm ready to smash the glass, Grandma steps into the room.

Chapter 26

Don't get me wrong – I'm grateful when Grandma opens the window, and it feels good to step inside on to the old rug, but this is the moment I've been dreading.

'Oh, Tom,' she says.

Jacob's cowering against the wall. He's holding my toothbrush out between him and Grandma. I stand in the middle of the room, staring at Grandma staring at Jacob. She doesn't look as shocked as I'd expect. Nor as angry.

The squirrel takes its chance and leaps out of the open window. Funny, it actually looks like a full-size squirrel now.

'Oh, Tom,' she says again. 'Who's this?'

'Jacob,' I say.

'The lad who's gone missing?'

I nod.

'Oh, Tom!' And then she laughs and sits back on the bed. 'I did wonder. The sheep, the donkey – what a racket it's been making – and the boats disappearing. You can shrink things – am I right?'

I nod.

'Fancy that – another shrinker in the family. I bet you didn't wish you could shrink things? Did you?'

I shake my head. I daren't speak.

'Exactly – very funny the way the whole thing works.'

'What works?' asks Jacob.

'The meteorite thing – the wishing thing – the village,' says Grandma, pushing the toothbrush to one side and staring at Jacob. 'It's a funny old place, Bywater-by-Sea. There are quite a few of us who've caught the meteorites, and not one of us got the thing we wished for.'

'You mean that there are more people like Tom wandering about? More nutters who can shrink things?'

'I certainly do,' says Grandma, tapping Jacob's huge stomach with a pencil. 'We can't all shrink things – we have different skills. There's Mr Albermarle, he floats – and Miss Darling...'

'Does she really have green fingers?'

Grandma nods. 'Oh yes, dear, she really does, and she really can make things grow awfully well. Miss Darling was in her father's greenhouse when the meteorite smashed through the glass, but I'm pretty sure she wished for Love. Eventually, a man from the Royal Plant Society came and inspected her garden, and they did fall in love – but it took twenty years.' Grandma smiles at the thought. 'And, there's Mr Albermarle. In case you've ever wondered – he is an inch or two off the ground. That's how he lays such beautiful concrete. Of course, he was at the airfield when the stone fell – and that's why he floats. He wished for work – and he got it, eventually. He's always in demand.'

We must be staring like we've no idea what she's talking about, because Grandma tries to explain it again. 'You see, the whole thing depends on where you are when you see the shooting star fall – you might wish for one thing, but your ability to get it will depend on where you are when you pick up your meteorite. If you were by the sea, for example, and you wished on a shooting star, and then picked it up, you might have wished for –' Grandma sees an empty sweet wrapper on the floor – 'chocolate...well, you wouldn't actually get chocolate, but you might get the ability to swim really well – and then, a few months later, you might win the Bywater Regis Swimming Cup, which as you know is entirely made of milk chocolate, or find yourself sponsored for the Olympics by a chocolate company. Do you see? So you sort of get your wish, but it just might take a while to happen.'

We stare at her, and I think about my wish – it could take years to happen.

'Oh – I get it,' says Jacob. 'That's why you two can shrink things. Your skill is all about making things small – cos you were in the model village when you saw it fall.' He glances from me to Grandma. 'But what did you actually wish for?'

'It's a secret,' I say, quickly.

'Fair enough, dear,' says Grandma. 'If it hasn't come true yet, you must keep it to yourself.' She looks at Jacob again, and frowns. 'So when did you get shrunk? Jacob.'

'Yesterday evening. Why?'

'I'll bet you started out smaller than this?'

Smaller?

Jacob stares about him. Eric's treasure chest is lying on the floor. We both look at it. I glance back at Jacob. He'd never fit in there. Surely? He couldn't have done.

'D'you mean he's growing?'

She nods. 'Look at your sheep out there – they're doing nicely.' She puts Jacob on the windowsill and gazes out at the model village.

I look at him. He's about six inches tall. He was about two inches and he should be four foot six. And there are the sheep, almost full-sized, waddling round the model village like footstools.

'All except for that one.' Grandma points at a single sheep skulking by the church.

'Why is that one smaller?' asks Jacob.

Grandma shrugs. 'I don't know. Growing's a funny thing – it's patchy. But most things do return to normal. More or less. There's nothing you can do to *make* them grow, nature just has to take its course.'

'So not everything grows back?' I ask, thinking of Jupiter and feeling sick again.

Grandma shakes her head. 'Some things stay small for ever. Some things only get halfway. Like I said, it's patchy.'

'But I'll be big again, won't I?' says Jacob, his voice extra squeaky. 'I'll be normal. Surely? Otherwise...'

There's a really long silence.

'Probably, dear. Almost certainly,' says Grandma, picking up the cardboard box full of miniature poos. 'It's perfectly true. You *are* growing. With any luck you'll get most of the way. It's just...it's not always 100% like it was before. Sometimes things are a little...lopsided. '

We both stare at Jacob. He stares at his hand. He looks terrified.

But Grandma's talking again. 'Anyway Tom – if, Jacob is

the worst of your crimes then we needn't worry too much. It's unfortunate, but not…catastrophic.'

'D'you mean am I the only thing he's shrunk?' Jacob glares at me.

'Nothing more important, I take it?' she asks.

There's a dangerously long silence, while I think about telling Grandma about Jupiter. But although I am now 99% worried about Jupiter, and only about 5% worried about Jacob, I'm still too scared to tell her. So I ask a question instead. 'Grandma, did you ever shrink anything – important?'

'I was lucky,' says Grandma. 'He grew back.'

'He?'

'Oh – "it" – I meant "it".' Grandma looks flustered. 'Not "he". Now, I must get on.' Grandma tilts her head to the side and smiles. But it isn't a full smile, it's the smile a grown-up does when they're trying to convince a child that everything's all right. She looks at Jacob. 'I'm sure you'll grow back in no time. You'll be fine; you'll see.'

'Will I?'

'Oh yes, love. Don't worry – I'm almost completely sure.'

She picks up a sock. 'Now, something's going on with

your sister, Tom, so I'll go back to the landing if you don't mind. I'm waiting for her to come home; I'd like a peek in her room. She's not let me in for a few days and the naughty girl's locked the door.' Grandma pushes herself up from the bed. 'She must have found a key in my bedroom. Something's up; I'm beginning to wonder if she can shrink things too.'

She opens the door.

'Grandma, what *did* you wish for?'

'Oh, it's silly, really – I wished for a baby brother. I wanted someone to play with.'

A baby? 'But...'

She steps out and closes the door.

I look down at Jacob. He's staring at his hand as if he's never seen it before. His face is completely white. And I know I shouldn't, but I can't help saying, 'Did you hear what she said – about things not always growing back?'

And for once, he doesn't say anything, just nods his head, and looks sick.

Chapter 27

Eric answers the door eventually. The shooting stars crash through the sky, crackling and spitting all around us. It's really warm too. Like Spain, not like Devon.

Jacob's so big his head sticks out of my pocket now. He hasn't said a word since Grandma. He keeps measuring himself against a pencil. I don't think he's grown in the last ten minutes though.

'Have you got it? Did you find it?' says Eric.

I shake my head. 'But I know where it is. It's in Tilly's room, and the thing is, Eric…it's growing.'

'Growing?'

I nod my head.

'Like – how much is it growing?'

'I don't know. Apparently, according to Grandma, most things grow back – look here.'

I lift Jacob out of my pocket. He sits on my hand. He's completely glum, and quite heavy. He's almost as long as the pencil now – although he resembles a pencil case more than anything else.

'Woah. Now that really is freaky,' says Eric.

'But Grandma says there's no way of knowing how big or how fast things will re-grow – or even if they'll grow back at all.'

'She said I'd grow back,' says Jacob.

'Probably,' I add. 'But I know Jupiter's getting bigger, because the magnetic pull's bigger – far more than five centimetres. It reaches right out into my bedroom,' I say, clinging to the only thing that's making me feel even 5% better. 'So that's good.'

'Hmmm. Getting from the size of a bead to the second largest body in the solar system is a long grow,' Eric says, staring up at the sky. 'Anyway, I need to look some stuff up on the computer – do some calculations. C'mon up – Dad's on the roof with the telescope. He thinks the meteor showers are signals from the mother ship. He's trying to make contact.'

We thunder up through the house, passing walls plastered with posters for science fiction films. I stop for breath by a newspaper article, framed on the wall.

There's a picture of Grandma, when she was about my age, and a child in a pushchair.

4th June 1962

Miraculous return of missing toddler

Stop Press — Today, at three o'clock, a child missing for more than two weeks was reunited with his ecstatic parents. On 1st May, toddler Colin Threepwood disappeared from his garden and it was presumed that he had wandered down to the sea and drowned. Police frogmen searched the bay, and surrounding countryside — but earlier today, he was found by young Amalthea Piper, wandering in the Bywater-by-Sea model village, none the worse for his ordeal. Miss Piper says she found him on the miniature bowling green, happy but hungry.

Police are baffled by his disappearance, and reappearance, and are reported to be following various leads. Police are also still looking into the complete disappearance of the tithe barn and the memorial horse trough, which took place on the same day.

Inspector Cyril Batson of the Bywater Regis CID dismissed the suggestion that the toddler and the barn were abducted by aliens as 'ridiculous'.

'See,' I say to Jacob. 'They didn't even believe him then.'

He says nothing, but sighs and climbs back up to sit in my pocket.

We follow Eric right up to the roof. There's a flat patch between two chimneys and it's amazing up here – you can see right over the town, to the sea. Eric's got his laptop set up, while his dad's standing next to an enormous telescope. Washing criss-crosses the roof, and all around, tinfoil flaps slightly in the breeze. Every surface is wrapped, even the chimney and the side roofs, like a giant Easter egg.

'What?'

'It's for signalling.' Eric points at massive bundle of wires lying in the corner of the roof. 'It's lined up, towards where Jupiter ought to be. When it's all ready, he'll turn the lights on, and kaboom.'

'Kaboom, what?' says Jacob.

'Kaboom, the aliens will be able to see us,' says Eric. 'They'll be able to follow the lines of lights to Dad.'

'You're serious?' asks Jacob.

Eric points at his dad.

I look up – for a second expecting to see an alien spaceship hovering above the house, but it's just the meteorites, bursting all around us. You can barely see the moon, let alone the stars. It's as if we're standing in a field of sparklers.

Eric's dad's waving his arms about like a little kid. 'Oh! It's them,' he says in this dreamy voice. 'It has to be, they're showing themselves at last. I mean, we might be walking between the worlds soon, Eric – taking on their mantle. And of course they took Jupiter as a sign.' He rubs his chin. 'Unless they took it for fuel.'

I can hear Jacob laughing in my pocket.

'Yes, Dad,' says Eric. He starts tapping things into his laptop. Strings of numbers fly across the screen.

'Oh yes – it's them. It must be, they're signalling, in such a sensitive way – so beautiful, so creative.'

'What's the telescope looking at?' I whisper.

Eric points at a square of black on one side of the laptop screen. 'That's the sky, that's what the telescope can see. It's trained to track Jupiter – at least, it's trained to track Jupiter's bit of empty sky.'

'Oh, yeah – sure, Grandson of Amalthea – have a look. You can be our witness, when we've gone.' I can see the excitement on his face. He's all dressed up in camouflage gear, like he's going on a jungle expedition. His hair's standing round his head like a halo. 'Eric – are you prepared, have you given up the Earth?'

I look at the little square of black on the laptop screen. All I can see is shooting stars. 'Gosh,' I say. 'Is there a spaceship?'

Eric's dad nods. 'It's probably the same one that visited me, the one that took me when I was little. Magical beings, huge gentle magical beings. They're so…cool.'

'Huge?' I ask.

'Oh yes, Grandson of Amalthea. Although I was only a year old, I remember them – giants from another world, giants that played with me and fed me and kept me warm. Giants that smelled of lavender. Giants, filled with love.'

Lavender? Grandma's meteorite was wrapped up with lavender, and what was it she said? *I wished for a baby brother to play with.*

Surely not – surely she didn't take Eric's dad? I stand with my mouth open, trying to form a sentence. 'So—'

But Eric interrupts. 'Jolly good, Dad, don't think Tom needs to know all this.' His voice squeaks with embarrassment.

'Of course not, that's in the past, and now we look to the future – are we ready to signal?' Eric's dad's hopping from foot to foot, gazing at the sky. Then he rushes over to an extension lead coming out of the roof trap. It's got twelve of those old yellowy plug sockets jammed in anyhow, and from those thirty or so more plugs, leading to the heap of wires at the side of the roof. It looks completely lethal.

His finger hovers over the little red switch.

I hold my breath.

Snap.

For just over half a minute, six lines of lights radiate out across the town, down to the sea, so that the roof looks like the control tower of a major international airport.

'Woah!' says Jacob.

'Oh, heavens!' cries Eric's dad, leaping in the centre. He crashes into a line of washing, and pants and socks float across the tinfoil. I step back – I don't want him to knock me flying – and I catch a whiff of something.

'What's that smell?' I whisper to Eric.

We turn, just in time to see a flame leap from the tangle of plugs, followed by a loud bang, and then we're plunged into darkness.

Chapter 28

We leave Eric trying to persuade his dad that without the lights, the aliens probably won't land, and that Eric might not be going with them if they do as he'd quite like to finish his education. His dad looks a bit gutted.

I take Jacob back down through the dark house and wait for Eric on the doorstep.

'So that's sorted, is it, Superboy? Snot Face has done the calculations, and we've got the all-clear to save the planet?'

He doesn't really fit in my pocket any more, but he's still small enough to squeeze to death. 'You haven't grown yet. You could spend the rest of your life in a devil suit, six inches tall.'

'Jupiter could spend the rest of our short lives in your sister's bedroom, only six inches across. You've got to find it, hope it grows and stick it back up where it's supposed to be. Let's face it, Genius, that's a lot of hoping.'

I stare up at the sky.

'You don't know how to put it back, though, do you?'

I shake my head. He's horribly right. 'Got any ideas?'

Jacob laughs. 'Oh – I love this, asking me for advice. Shame we'll all be dead before I get to tell anyone.'

We stumble down the street. Eric's panting hard. He's got his laptop weighing him down and I don't think he's used to this much exercise, but I need him with me. He's the only person I know who's remotely capable of putting Jupiter back where it should be.

'If we can get Jupiter back in the right place, really soon,' says Eric, 'all the shooting stars'll stop. The asteroids'll go back to where they came from.'

'Sure?'

'100%.'

'100%?' I ask.

'1000%,' says Eric.

We're nearly back at the model village and this time I can see the glow from Tilly's bedroom. I hope that's not the planet. It's been nearly three days – so how big will it be now? A tennis ball, a football? Maybe even a space hopper.

The garage door's open. Dad's hammering on the door

of the disappearing cabinet. There are rabbits bouncing around his feet. 'Laura? Laura? Can you hear me? I'll try this one.'

'Dad?'

'I've lost your mum inside. We can't find the proper door. Give me a hand.' He looks a bit desperate.

'I'd love to, Dad – but we're on a mission. Back soon.'

Grandma's still sitting there on the landing, knitting. She's knitting a chessboard now. Tilly's door's shut.

Grandma looks up. 'Hello, Tom, Eric.'

'Is Tilly back?' I ask.

She peers at my pocket. 'Jacob. My, haven't you grown. Yes, she is back, but she sneaked in while I was trying to help your father find your mother in the disappearing cabinet. Your mother seems to have properly disappeared. And now Tilly's locked herself in.'

I hammer on the door.

'Tilly – let me in. I know what you took – but I don't think you know what it is.'

'What is it she's got, dear?' asks Grandma.

'Nothing much.'

Jacob jabs me in the neck.

'Ow – no, really, nothing much.'

'Go away,' shouts Tilly. 'I'm having fun and I don't want you wrecking it.'

'Tilly – please.'

'There's a password.'

'Please?' I shout.

'No.'

'Abracadabra,' calls Grandma.

'Halloween,' says Eric.

'Woodland Friends?' I say.

'No, no, no.'

'Shazam, what is it that they say at the pantomime?' says Grandma. 'Open sesame.'

'Doctor Who!' I shout, grabbing the TV pages from Grandma's knitting bag. I take them apart and slip a sheet under the door.

'Rumplestiltskin.'

'Guinea pig, hamsters.' I lift Jacob up and put him on the door handle. 'Dressing up, wings, wands, sparkly crowny things.'

'What am I doing here?' whispers Jacob.

I point into the lock, at the shiny end of the key. 'Push it out.'

'Aladdin!' yells Grandma.

'No and utterly, no.'

'Please,' I say.

'You've already said that; and it's wrong.'

Jacob's reaching around inside the lock. He waves his hands at us, as if we should shout louder, so we do.

'CINDERELLA,' yells Grandma, really loudly.

'FAIRY,' I scream.

'E = MC squared,' shouts Eric.

We all stare at him.

'Theory of relativity,' says Eric, looking at the floor.

'Oooooh,' says Jacob, his leg deep in the keyhole.

Ping. The key falls from the lock on to the newspaper and quick as a flash I pull it under the door.

'Very clever, I'm sure,' says Grandma, taking the key from me and slipping it past Jacob's leg, into the lock.

The door opens.

Oh!

Chapter 29

I was prepared for the idea that Jupiter would have grown. I was expecting something the size of a basketball. But this?

'Wow,' says Eric.

'Oh my word,' says Grandma, sinking on to the bed.

'Go away,' says Tilly. 'It's mine, and I want you all to go away.'

We stand there, staring. Even Jacob stops with his mouth open, gazing at the giant ball. It's an Eric tall and an Eric wide. Spinning like the display in the jeweller's in the high street, but there's no glitter any more – instead it's sort of smoking, like hot brown soup.

'Tilly,' says Grandma. 'What is it?'

Tilly doesn't say anything, but points at me.

Grandma stares at me. 'Tom?'

I shrug – what else can I do? And then, when Grandma goes on staring, I say, 'Jupiter. It's Jupiter.'

For a moment, I think she's going to have a heart attack. 'Tom,' she says. 'Tom. What have you done?'

'I shrank it. Three days ago.'

'No! I can't believe you're that stupid.'

'But, Grandma, I didn't know. It was the first thing I clicked on.'

'You should have told me.'

CRACK.

The planet groans and almost doubles in size. Now it's a Dad tall and a Dad wide.

'Now look what you've done!' shouts Tilly. 'It's wrecking my room.'

'S'not my fault!' I shout.

'Yes it is,' says Tilly. 'It's all your fault.'

'Oh, goody goody, are you two going to have a fight? I love a good fight.'

'Who said that?' Tilly, who's been looking for a sulking spot on the other side of the room, sees Jacob.

'Oh, wow, a living doll.' She leaps forward and grabs him from the floor. 'It's a real doll, just you wait. You can live with Toots in the Spangle Palace. And I've got some clothes for you.'

'No, stop her!'

'Oh! Shush, Jacob, can't you see it's a crisis?' says Grandma.

Eric picks his way over the scattered Woodland Friends, until his fingers are an inch from the planet's surface. 'Wow!' He's gazing at it. 'Wow.'

'Don't. It'll burn you,' I say.

'One hundred and sixty degrees below freezing,' he says in answer, his voice full of hushed wonder. 'It's incredible. It's marvellous.'

'Probably...'

'I never thought... I mean, we're standing in the presence of an ancient and wonderful thing, something that's reached out to man for as long as man's been on the planet.'

'Eric, you're beginning to sound like your father,' says Grandma.

'Sorry... There are sixty-four moons, you know. Look – there, see.'

Something about the size of a ping-pong ball whizzes past my nose.

'It takes a little under ten hours to rotate.'

'Help! Snot Face, Model Village, help!'

I turn to look for Jacob, but there's this cracking noise,

and the whole thing grows again, taking a chunk out of the ceiling.

'Yow!' screams Tilly, and grabs Jacob to her chest. She's jammed him into a pair of mauve flared trousers, and a velveteen jacket. He's trying to get his teeth round her finger, but Tilly's used to hamsters. There's no way she'll let him bite her.

I look at the planet, huge, and I look at the door, tiny. Then I look at our team.

We're all useless. We've got a lippy miniature devil, my stupid sister, an old lady and Eric.

Together

Everyone

Achieves

More.

TEAM. Well, it doesn't work with planets.

And it occurs to me, that no one – ever in the history of the world – has had to deal with this problem.

There's another cracking sound and Jupiter grows *again*, but there's nowhere for it to go now, just the ceiling.

We all step back a pace.

CRACK.

The planet swells again and we step back another pace.

There's a kind of gap showing underneath, but the top's

gone right up into the roof space. I can see a blue suitcase revolving on the top.

It ought to be funny, but it isn't.

Half the planet's in the room, and half's in the attic. It's broken right through the rafters; all that's holding it in is the roof itself.

Eric picks up a pair of fairy wings from the floor and pokes Jupiter. It rolls and bounces like a tennis ball on water. 'Helium,' he says. 'It's trying to get out.'

A second later, and I've got one foot on Eric's head the other on one of Grandma's travelling trunks and I'm tearing slates off the roof and chucking them into the garden.

'Thing is,' shouts Eric. 'We don't want it to take off. It needs to be launched.'

'What do you mean?' I say, tipping a bird's nest out of the gutter. 'How do we launch a thing this big?'

'No idea — but don't let it get away. We can't leave it bumbling along over Earth, it might end up in the wrong place.'

I climb up above Jupiter, and look dismally at the beams holding the slates up. I'd need to get rid of at least two beams to make a hole big enough to put it through, and that would only work if the planet didn't have another growing spurt.

'Have you got a saw, Grandma?'

'Your dad's got it, for the disappearing box – for goodness' sake, Tom, hurry up. If it gets any bigger it'll destroy the whole house.'

How on earth am I supposed to do this?

I push against the beams. I can't possibly do anything with these, they're rock hard.

I stare up at the fountains of shooting stars breaking overhead and put my thumb and middle finger together.

Yes.

Yes. I can sort this out.

I climb out on to the roof slates. It's horribly high, but I try not to think about that. The planet's nudging the beams, bouncing against them.

I stand back from the beams as far as I can.

Click

Click

And for good measure. Click.

Three small bars of wood lie in the palm of my hand.

Yes!

But the planet's trying to get out now – it's as if it's alive, trying to find a way through the gap. So I put my foot on it. It's the only thing I can do.

'Help!' I shout.

'Tom?' calls Eric. 'Is it free? Could it float away?'

'Almost,' I say, watching the sole of my shoe crack in the sub-zero temperature and wondering how long I can stand here. 'I need something to hold it with, before my foot falls off.'

'Hang on there.' Eric stuffs Tilly's cuddly penguin up through the hole. It's about the same height as Grandma, in lime green. 'Use this to hold it, and we'll get blankets – and ropes.'

I jam the penguin on top of the planet and clamp it down with my frozen shoe… Ice crystals form on the green fluff and creep towards my foot. There's about a beak left before the ice reaches me. I look down through the hole for Eric. But all I can see is Jacob being dressed by Tilly. He's now about the size of a large baby, and he's wearing one of Tilly's pink babygros.

'HELP!' I shout down the hole.

Jacob looks up at me, mournfully. 'I would if I could,' he says. His little arms flap on either side, he's powerless against her. I almost feel sorry for him.

'Here,' calls Eric. 'Take this.' He pushes something through the rafters. 'I'll come round to the front of the house.'

'Is that my fairy bedspread you're destroying, Tom?' Tilly's voice floats up.

I sling the bedspread over the penguin and the planet. Four ropes hang down from the corners. Jupiter drops slightly, as if the weight of the blanket is just enough to stop it flying away. I throw the ropes over the front of the house.

Phew.

CRACK.

As if someone's just pumped it full of fresh helium, the planet bounces back up at me.

NO!

I press both my hands into Tilly's fairy bedspread, and they sink into the surface. It feels utterly strange, like a vast lump of frozen candyfloss. Swelling, frozen candyfloss.

'Hurry up!' I shout.

There's shouting and banging and screams from Tilly and doors slamming below and then Eric yells up at me from the garden. 'We've got a ladder – hang on!'

The ropes stretch and the planet starts to slide neatly out of the attic and over the last few shattered tiles. It teeters on the edge of the roof.

'Woah!' shouts Eric. 'That's big – that's mega big.'

He's right. The planet's grown massively in the last few minutes and is now about the size of a small hot air balloon. It's pulling upwards like a hot air balloon too, but we don't have any of those net things that they hang over balloons, or a handy basket or a licence to fly large round things over Devon.

My arms ache from pushing it downwards, and the bedspread's starting to crack from the cold.

'MOO!'

Eric, Grandma and a random cow stare up at me. Eric and Grandma hang on to the ropes, but Grandma's feet have already left the ground.

There's shouting, and a squeal from Tilly, and Jacob rushes out into the garden, the torn babygro flapping around his feet. He grabs the end of another rope and immediately his feet bounce over the miniature war memorial.

We need more help or more weight.

Mum and Dad?

But Mum's stuck in the disappearing cabinet, and Dad's crashing about trying to get her out.

I look down. 'Tilly!'

Her face appears through the hole. 'What!'

'Get a blanket from the sofa and hand it up to me, quick.'

'No. I'm tidying my bedroom.'

'Come on, Tilly, please.'

'What's it worth?'

'Tilly!' shouts Grandma from below. 'Go and get the big quilt off my bed. Now!'

'Hey!' shouts Jacob. 'My feet are off the ground. I'm flying!'

There's an age of silence and then I hear thumping from the room below and Tilly opens her window. She's got Grandma's giant patchwork quilt. She won't hurry; she's sulking, I can tell from the way she moves. She's gazing out at Jacob like he was the sweetie she lost.

CRACK.

The planet swells again, and my feet bounce on the roof.

'Tilly! Hand it up here.'

'No!'

CRACK.

'Please.'

'I won't. You're silly,' and she pulls her head back in and goes back into her room.

'Jacob!' I shout at him. 'Do something, please.'

'What?'

'She loves you. She thinks you're a giant baby – do something.'

'You've got to be joking. Why would I do that?'

'Because you might just want to do the right thing. Because you might want to play a part in saving the planet?'

There's a long silence while we pant and tug and scrabble, trying to hold Jupiter in check.

'Because that would make me a nicer person?'

'It would.'

I can practically hear his brain working.

'Cooee – Tilly, you help us with the blanket, and I promise you can play with me afterwards.' And then he mutters, 'I'll kill you for this.'

'Really?' says Tilly and throws open her window again.

'Come on, let's put the blankets on the big sparkly ball, and then when we've put it back into space, you can tuck me into bed.'

'I know it's Jupiter, stupid,' says Tilly. 'But if you'll really play with me, afterwards?'

'Promise.'

'Promise, double promise, with bells on?'

'Promise, double promise, with bells on,' growls Jacob.

Woah.

'Well,' says Tilly, 'if you really mean it.' She turns and stuffs the corner of the quilt up through the hole in the roof. It weighs a ton. It's so heavy that when I finally get it over the planet, the planet starts to sink. It slides slowly down the front of the house, like a huge blob of ice cream.

CRACK. The planet doubles in size.

'Yeay!' shouts Jacob. 'Now we can all be crushed to death.'

Chapter 30

I scramble down through the hole into Tilly's room. She's picking up her scattered Woodland Friends.

'Thanks,' I say.

'I'm never helping you again,' she says, without looking. But she follows me downstairs and when I grab the fourth corner of the quilt, she joins me.

'Are we just going to let it go and let the astro-whatsits sort it out?' pants Jacob.

Eric starts pulling hard, lugging the planet and the rest of us over the rooftops of the model village. 'No – we're going to fire it. We need to get it against the south-western sky, get it between the church tower and the castle bailey and fire it.'

CRACK.

'Fire it?' I ask.

'Yes – like a catapult,' says Eric, panting, his laptop bag swinging round his neck.

'Are you serious?'

A giant catapult? That would need a giant elastic band.

CRACK.

And then the lights come on.

'It's Dad!' cries Eric. 'He's fixed the wiring.'

A line of yellow bulbs spring into life, one by one. They ping on, stretching straight across the model village, and race out towards the sea. Another line starts out at the real castle and pings back towards the centre of town, and Eric's house.

The town's cut into sections with the lines of lights.

The gate clangs behind us. 'Guys, I was looking for you – woah! What's this? What goes down?' It's Eric's dad; he seems to be wearing pyjamas. Actually I don't care what he's wearing – he's tall and heavy and I'm really glad to see him.

'It's Jupiter, Dad,' says Eric.

'Oh – yeah – sure, fantastic. A giant planet in the model village, that so proves the thinness of the Veil.'

The great thing about Eric's dad is that he'll believe anything.

CRACK.

How brilliant is that?

'Hold on here, Dad,' shouts Eric. 'Take over from Tom.' His dad grabs the quilt, I let go, and they stumble on towards the model village castle. They're all flapping from the sides, Jacob swinging like a blue tit from a giant peanut feeder.

By the shed there's a hosepipe; I pull on it. It's long enough, but not really stretchy.

I run on, thinking about stretchy things.

YUK!

It's one of the pumpkin lanterns, almost back to full size.

Pulling my shoe out of the goo, I rush towards the house. Something's blocking the hallway. The donkey. It's donkey sized and it's got Grandma's apron in its mouth.

I squeeze past it and run up the stairs. From the landing you almost wouldn't know there's a massive hole in the roof. Diving into Mum and Dad's room I throw open their wardrobe and gaze at the shelves.

There's Mum's glittery swimming costume, and her diamond-studded hats. But on the top shelf are braces. Hundreds of pairs of braces.

Dad wants to use them for performing, but I think they've got a higher purpose.

I count thirty pairs, and fill my arms with them. The donkey's still standing in the hall, eating the coat stand, but I wriggle out of the front door, trails of elastic flapping all around me.

The others are still fighting their way through the model village. Jupiter's even bigger. Surely everyone in the village can see this. Everyone in Devon. Everyone in England. Everyone in Europe. Maybe everyone in the world?

I run to overtake them and smash into something heavy and plastic. It's the giant hot dog from the seafront. Very big and very hard.

'Ow!'

I reach the castle just before the others and discover that there is no clever way of attaching one pair of braces to another. I just have to tie them all up, like a load of spaghetti. They hang like a long, badly made hammock, slack between the castle and the church, illuminated by the shooting stars bursting overhead.

I pull on them. Together they're strong and stretchy and I feel 7%, maybe 10% better.

'Mind out – here we come!' yells Jacob.

I turn and grab the bottom of his rope. He's dangling above me, like a small piece of ballast in a shredded babygro. He's growing. Shame – small was beautiful.

CRACK.

Jupiter swells again; in a few minutes we'll have lost it. I feel the slope of the castle under my feet, and hook my toes into one of the windows of the great tower.

CRACK.

'Eric! The catapult's ready,' I yell.

'I just need to check something.' Eric drops to the ground and paces back towards the house. He balances his laptop on the miniature amusement arcade and punches in some more numbers.

The planet pulls again, and I wrap the rope around my hand. If it goes it's going to take me with it.

'Oh, Amalthea, this is truly wondersome,' says Eric's dad. He's clambering up the side, like some sort of mad mountain climber, but it's keeping the planet down.

'Hurry up, Snot Face!' yells Jacob.

'Who was that?' Tilly drops on to the path. 'Oh no! Where's my doll gone?' She sees Jacob. 'Ugh – yuk, you're horrible, Jacob Devlin, and you've ruuuuuined that babygro. You were lying – all boys are liars. I should never have trusted you.'

CRACK.

'Tilly, dear, now's not the moment. Grab my feet, hang on,' says Grandma.

But Tilly won't, she just sticks her nose in the air and stomps back towards the house.

'I'm going to let go,' I yell. 'Hook your feet into the castle windows.'

'Righty ho!' shouts Grandma, jamming her substantial feet into the main entrance of the miniature castle and steadying the planet.

I let go, and without my weight the whole thing bounces up, but then settles back down.

I run towards Eric, glancing back to see Jupiter hanging over the castle, Grandma and Jacob flapping against the sides. Eric's dad's balancing on top. Jacob's got one hand wrapped round the flagpole, the other gripping the quilt.

Something suddenly occurs to me.

'Eric – does Jupiter have a top and bottom, a north and south pole?'

He stares at me, the shooting stars reflecting in his glasses.

'Well, yes.'

'So which way up is it now?'

He peers at it. 'I think it might be sideways. The red spot, the storm, is supposed to be at the bottom.'

I gaze at the planet, I can't see the red spot – it might even be upside down.

'Jacob – red spot at the bottom!' I shout.

Jacob peers under the quilt and shouts something to Grandma; Grandma leans forward to listen and lets go.

Jupiter springs up.

'Ahhhrgh!' screams Jacob and falls off.

Jupiter bounces up, but Eric's dad stands there, silhouetted against the shooting stars, his arms out on either side. He's surfing the planet.

He looks like he's enjoying it.

'It's the wrong way up, Dad,' shouts Eric.

'What? Oh yeah – wow, this is CRAZY.' He walks on the ball, like a performing dog. Eric's mad dad walks the planet round so that the red spot is at the bottom. While he does it, the whole thing's floating up.

Eric and I run to the tangle of elastic and pull it downwards and backwards until it's at full stretch.

'We need to get Jupiter back in here, like it's a missile,' I shout.

CRACK.

Grandma and Jacob push at the planet, which bobs over until it nestles inside the curve of the elastic. It only just fits between the towers on either side.

Without Eric's dad on top, it would float away. He's keeping it down and keeping it steady.

'Wow,' he cries.

'Jump!' I shout.

'It's fine, it's cool. This is massive, this is better than aliens,' says Eric's dad.

'But we're going to send it back into space.'

'Leave him be, love – he's enjoying himself,' says Grandma.

'I don't know where we're sending it,' whispers Eric.

'What?' I say.

'Hurry up,' says Grandma.

'I can't see the right stars – I don't know where to put it.'

CRACK.

There's a horrible silence, while I can practically hear Eric thinking.

'Follow the lights,' I say.

'What?'

'Follow your dad's lights – they point towards Jupiter. He's lined them up.'

Eric's silent for a moment.

'You're absolutely right, that's it.'

'Sure?'

'100%,' says Eric.

'100%?' I look up. The sky's busting with stars, and shooting stars.

'Yes – I'm 100% sure. Let's just do it.'

'He's sure!' shouts Jacob. 'Just get on with it!'

'And believe,' shouts Grandma. 'It's most important that we all believe.'

'I believe,' says Eric.

'And me,' yells Jacob from the flagpole.

I close my eyes. Open them again, and believe as hard as I can. 'One. Two. Three…'

Kerrrrrtwannnnnng.

Chapter 31

It's wild, really. It's crazy. One minute Jupiter was there, rolling over the model village, all of us shouting and screaming and falling over the houses – the next it was gone. We looked up there, forty-three minutes later, and there it was – twinkling in the sky, framed by the shooting stars, and perfectly in line with Eric's dad's landing lights.

And we'd done it.

Just like that, we'd saved the Earth.

We stood in the garden for a long time waiting for Eric's dad. Then we set out to look for him. I didn't think we'd sent him off with Jupiter, but I wasn't sure because things were a bit panicky with the braces.

I kept imagining him up there, floating about on the edge of the giant planet, and it worried me. If I was Eric, I wouldn't like to think of my dad loose in the cosmos, especially my dad, a thousand times bigger, or a million times bigger.

We started walking towards the sea; we found the bedspread on the crazy golf course, and the quilt on the seafront.

But no sign of Eric's dad.

We searched for hours until Grandma came over and put her hand on Eric's shoulder. 'Time to go to bed now, love.'

Eric looked gutted, and Grandma tried to comfort him. Even Jacob held his hand, like a mad waddling baby in the high street.

'He'll be fine,' said Grandma. 'Honestly, just you wait.'

But I don't think she was sure, and I think she was the most surprised of all of us when he suddenly appeared, wet and giggling from the sea. He couldn't speak properly, just kept saying:

'Wow.'

'Wow,' and,

'Yeah.'

Then he said:

'Cosmic.'

And 'Wow!' again.

Eric held his hand really tight. And Grandma started to sing 'Rock-a-bye-baby'.

She put her arm around him, and called him her little one.

So we all walked back together. The geek, his mad dad, the half-size devil, the old lady and me. We giggled all the way back to the house, and when we got there, Grandma made hot chocolate with lumpy cocoa powder and off milk.

Nothing ever tasted so good.

Epilogue

Today's my birthday and only one of my scary dreams has come true. Mum and Dad did do a 'Mr and Mrs Magic' show at school. Grandma tried to stop them, but Mr Devlin was so pleased to have Jacob back, even though he was only four foot tall, he said we should have a big celebration, so we did. It wasn't too awful. Mum shut Dad in the cabinet this time, and he managed to get out after a while, although the audience thought it was hilarious. The girls loved the rabbits, and the pigeons pooed all over the dining hall.

Mum and Dad bought me a telescope for my birthday, and I've promised Eric that I'll never be tempted to click anything through it. Grandma gave me a real camera; she said it might stop any accidents.

She's making a cake for tea, and we're all going to have

a twilight picnic on the beach, cos even though Jupiter's back, it's still pretty warm. I'm mixing the butter and the sugar; Jacob's outside with Eric and his dad, stringing the landing-strip lights all over the model village. It's going to look crazy when they all get switched on at sunset. That's in about ten minutes. I wonder if tiny aliens'll land on the tiny version of Eric's house?

I jam the spoon into the buttery lumps and try to squash them against the side of the bowl and we work in silence, listening to the sounds from the garden.

Grandma lays down the flour sieve. 'Tell me something, Tom. What did you wish for?'

'That's a secret,' I say.

'But has it come true?'

I look out of the kitchen window at Jacob, holding a string of lights up to Eric's dad. Eric, feeding carrots to the donkey, and even Tilly chasing rabbits around the model village. They're all my friends.

And I think about my wish.

'Yes, Grandma – it really has.'

SHRUNK!

From an original idea by Rufus Mckay

Acknowledgements

I would like to thank the very many people who helped bring this book to life.

Ian, for listening, suggesting, reading, cooking a great many meals and generally egging me on.

Rufus, for a moment of brilliance on Swanage Pier.

Rosa, for loving Sylvanians.

My friends and my family, for giving endless support.

My compatriots and tutors on the Bath Spa Writing for Young People MA, for teaching me to be a better writer.

Gill and Sarah for thinking that SHRUNK! 'had legs'.

G.G. for encouragement.

Sara O'Connor, whose tenacity and love of this story has brought us to this point.

Georgia Murray for ironing out the bumps.

The new team at Hot Key Books, who have given it the energy and spark that I hope it deserves.

But finally,

I'd like to thank Kate Shaw and Pippa le Quesne, my fantastic agents, for showing extraordinary faith.

A few things you might like to know about Jupiter

Jupiter is a pretty special place. Just as Eric says in the story, it has a lot of moons, so if you could stand on the surface of the planet – which you couldn't because it's too cold and made of gas – you'd be surrounded by moons rising and falling like a merry-go-round. He's also right about the red spot. The *Great Red Spot* is a storm and it has been observed for more than 300 years, but there's another one forming – yes, you got it right – it's called the *Little Red Spot*.

Jupiter is so big that the diameter (the line right through the middle of a sphere) of the planet is approximately 142,984 kilometres. So if you set out in a cosmic camper van (with some sandwiches), driving at a top speed of 80 kilometres an hour, it would take you 74 days to drive through all the helium, liquid hydrogen and maybe some lumps of rock, and then out the other side. In comparison, the same camper van, after a service, would take only a week to drive through the Earth's core, and you'd be in Australia in time for lunch on the last day, having covered roughly 12,756 kilometres. And if you wanted to cross from the dark to the light side of our Moon, it would take a mere 44 hours, so you might even be home by bedtime on the second day.

Although we can see Jupiter from the Earth, even without a telescope, but probably with the help of someone who knows which of the bright starlike things it is, it's a reeeeeeeeally long way away. At its closest the distance is 628,743,036 kilometres, which in the cosmic camper van travelling at 80 kilometres an hour would take 327,470 days or 897 years. So if you bothered to set out, you'd need to take a shedload of sandwiches to keep you going, and probably, by the time you got there, it would have moved on. And you'd be really old.

For more information about Jupiter and the rest of the solar system, use the internet to find planetariums, local astronomical societies, stargazing events, and look up NASA and National Space Centres to find exciting information about space exploration, and on a clear night, get away from the street lights, and look up.

It's amazing.

A little bit about F.R. Hitchcock

I grew up loving model villages.

The first one I fell in love with was Godshill in the Isle of Wight. I explored it and invented people to live in it, animals to run in the tiny patchwork fields, stories to fill the streets. I took those ideas home and went on playing with the imaginary people in my own imaginary model village. I never forgot about them.

Years later, I was supposed to have grown up. I went away to university and studied English, but spent my whole time in the drama studio building sets and messing about with scale. Working life came my way, but I still managed to bring the model village with me. I sold Applied Art, which means 3D things, and we had a shop underneath the gallery, where we sold beautiful wooden toys. A lot of them were miniatures, and I lost myself arranging them into scenes, re-creating snapshots from my imaginary model village. When my children came along, they wanted railway tracks laid out. I obliged, but the best bit was arranging the people, the houses, the cows, and then, when they were older, I introduced them to their first model village and – much to my delight – they too were captivated.

Then one summer we had a damp family holiday in Swanage. Driven by wind and rain to Corfe Castle, the magical world of SHRUNK! revealed itself and the characters, just as they had when I was little, jumped out from the miniature houses and the rainbeaten castle.

SHRUNK! was born.

I like to visit a model village at least once a year. You can do the same. Wikipedia is a good place to find them all – they're scattered all over the world.

Find out more about F.R.Hitchcock at:

www.hotkeybooks.com

http://fleurhitchcock.wordpress.com

twitter@murhilltypist

SHRUNK! is a work of fiction. I've done my very best to check all my facts but if you think I've got anything wrong I'd love to hear from you.